SHIPLEY MANOR

TIM WALKER

ff

faber and faber

First published in 2007
by Faber and Faber Limited
3 Queen Square London WC1N 3AU

Typeset by Faber and Faber
Printed in England by
Mackays of Chatham, Chatham, Kent

The right of Tim Walker to be identified as author of this
work has been asserted in accordance with Section 77 of
the Copyright, Designs and Patents Act 1988

A CIP record for this book
is available from the British Library

ISBN 978–0–571–23284–0
ISBN 0–571–23284–1

To my shipmates
Jo, Jessica, Sarah and Samuel

Welcome to Shipley Manor Country Club

We would like to draw the attention of all new members to the following club rules:

1. Members and their guests must use one of the treadmills before entering the club building.

2. Magic Fizzle may only be purchased from the bar; it may not be drunk directly from the moat.

3. Any slugs encountered in the gardens must be handed over to Slugbucket, the gardener.

4. A Shipley Manor Jumblupp judge must referee all Jumblupp league games.

5. Do not be scared of the animals. Yes, they talk, but that passes for normal here.

Finally, we would remind all club members that rules are made to be broken.

Thank you for your co-operation
The Management

Shipmate Wanted

Young person required to keep holiday cabins
shipshape. Flexible hours and free Fizzle
for the right candidate. Apply to the Captain,
Shipley Manor Country Club, Shipley.

Tom Sterling's father wished him good luck and dropped him off in the gravel car park outside the estate. Tom thanked him politely, then watched their old car disappear over the hill, before crunching his way towards the huge iron gates which stood locked across the entrance to the driveway. They stretched far above Tom's head and were topped with an elegant arch in which the words 'Shipley Manor' had been twisted and hammered into shape by a master ironmonger centuries before. The gates were hung between two brick gateposts, each of which had a king-sized stone pineapple perched on top. Roger, Tom's father, had been very impressed by these and had admired them for several minutes. He'd explained to Tom that in the eighteenth century pineapples were the rarest and most expensive food you could eat, so 'the great and good' as he respectfully called them, often put stone pineapples on top of their gateposts as a symbol of their wealth and power. You'd soon break a tooth trying to eat one of those, though, thought Tom.

On either side of the gates an ancient ivy-clad wall stretched as far as the eye could see, and set into the wall, just to the left of the gates, was a small wooden door. Its peeling red paint so perfectly matched the weathered old bricks that Tom almost missed it, but the hand-painted sign alongside drew his attention . . . and presented him with something of a dilemma. It read:

Enter how you like, shipmates,
Through the door or over the gates

Tom looked longingly at the gates, hesitating. Then he walked through the doorway.

Like any normal boy, Tom would have enjoyed climbing over the gates. But he couldn't do it, no matter what the sign said. You see, Tom was a particularly well-behaved and serious boy, whose life was governed by endless rules. In Tom's 'don't do this' and 'don't do that' world, grass was for not walking on, walls were for not sitting on and gates were definitely for *not* climbing on. So even though the sign was, in fact, inviting him to clamber up the ironwork, it still seemed wrong. Besides, he told himself, he was wearing his best trousers. A dirty mark on those and another rule would have been broken. So through the door he went.

Tom's life had been like this ever since his mother died. He was four when it happened. She had drowned saving someone else's life, a 'rule-breaker' as his father called him. The three of them had gone to the seaside one summer's day and had just finished building a sandcastle together. It was hot work, so Tom and his father had set off barefoot along the promenade in search of ice-creams. While they were gone, a man decided to go for a swim, despite an official red warning flag on the beach telling him not to. He got into trouble almost immediately. The strong undercurrent swept him out to sea and Tom's mother, who happened to be a very good swimmer, plunged in after him. By the time she reached him he was almost drowning, so she kept him afloat until the lifeboat arrived. But the effort must have exhausted her, and when the coastguard pulled the two of them out of the water, the man was alive, but Tom's mother wasn't. Although Tom could recall seeing her photograph afterwards in the local newspaper, the *Shipley Gazette*, his most vivid memory of that time was a smell. On the day of his mother's funeral the biggest, most beautiful bunch of flowers had arrived at his house. His father had read the tag, then taken the flowers outside and stuffed them head-first into the dustbin, slamming the metal lid on after them with a deafening crash. After the funeral Tom had sneaked outside to take a look. Even now he could remember the sickly-sweet smell as he lifted the lid, and although he was barely old enough to read, he recognised the name on the tag. It was the same one as in the newspaper. The flowers were from the man in the sea, the 'rule-breaker'.

After that his father had become quite ill. He couldn't get up in the mornings, or shave, or do his job at Shipley Bank. More importantly, he couldn't look after Tom. So Tom had gone to stay with his grandparents for a time, whilst his father recovered.

When Tom returned home his father had changed. He was extremely clean-shaven and stood straighter than before, with his shoulders pressed back as though he were carrying an invisible football between his shoulder blades. He had taken to going on long runs before breakfast, and to the gym every evening. He had also gone back to work. Each day he would set off in a crisp white shirt, perfectly ironed tie, his new pin-stripe suit – which had creases down the legs so sharp you could chop vegetables with them – and shoes that he polished every night, sometimes twice, before going to bed. Weekends were spent keeping their small semi-detached house in perfect order. In the kitchen, cups and saucers sat stacked with military precision, their handles aligned as if awaiting inspection. In the garden, no daisy dared trespass on the flat, green, perfectly manicured lawn. Tom's father had made a decision. He and Tom would survive the future together by being healthy, hard-working, sensible and self-disciplined. Above all, unlike the man in the sea, Tom would learn the importance of what he called 'the three Rs': Rules, Responsibility and Respect for authority. And he had. And that's why Tom didn't climb the gates that morning. He just knew it wasn't right.

Tom began his descent of the long, sloping driveway to Shipley Manor. The first thing he came to was a green wooden box which hung from the top of an old fence post. 'News and Post' was painted in white letters on its lid, and it reminded Tom that he'd brought the advert from the *Shipley Gazette* with him, just in case he needed to show it to someone. It seemed the sensible thing to do. He put his hand in his pocket to double-check it was still there, then carried on walking.

The driveway was in poor repair. It was peppered with dozens of potholes, some small enough to twist your ankle in, others like mini-craters, the sort that make big, splashy puddles when it rains. Tom tiptoed around each one – careful to avoid any mishap which might dirty his best clothes before his interview. Either side of him, trees and bushes stretched far above his head, meeting in the middle to form a dark, leafy tunnel. Although it wasn't raining the spring air was damp and slightly misty, and every few yards a water droplet would slip off a new leaf and land with a cold 'plop' on Tom's head, forcing him to run his fingers through his fair hair just to check it was only water, and not something altogether more unpleasant. As he walked, Tom imagined how much spookier the driveway would be at night, so although he didn't believe in ghosts or any other nonsense like that, he was quite glad to see a patch of light up ahead. As he came closer he saw that it was a break in the trees, beyond which two sheep were grazing in a field of thick grass. One of the sheep looked up and saw Tom. It ambled over to the fence which separated them and faced him, chewing.

'Hello, young man,' it said.

Tom jumped back in surprise. He looked around, expecting to see another person near by, but there was no one. He and the sheep were alone, and the sheep was staring at him, as if expecting a reply. A hot and prickly feeling started to creep up Tom's back. Something wasn't right here. He opened his mouth to say hello, which would have been the polite thing to do after all, but then he shut it again. He couldn't allow himself to do anything so ridiculous – talking animals, like witches and wizards, fairies and hobgoblins, only existed in books that he found far too silly to read. There had to be another explanation – a proper one. Perhaps he'd imagined it, or misheard it, or maybe he was still in bed dreaming. But when he pinched himself on the arm, the sharp pain convinced him that he was very much awake, and he decided there was only one thing to do, and that was to worry about it . . . later. In the meantime he had a job interview not to be late for, so he left the sheep behind him and quickened his pace down the steep, meandering driveway.

Finally, he rounded the last bend and saw Shipley Manor for the first time.

The magnificent country house was bathed in dazzling sunlight. Tom blinked, and for one hazy moment the house appeared to be floating in the centre of the countryside like an enormous stone ship. It stood at the top of a narrow, lush valley, protected on three sides by a steep wooded slope which curved half-way round it like a bowl. Tom had descended the slope slightly to one side of the house. From here, like Shipley Manor itself, he had a clear view down the valley to the sea, which he could just make out, shimmering sunnily in the distance.

Although Shipley Manor was most definitely a house, in many ways it did in fact resemble a ship. The windows on all three floors were round, like portholes. At the front of the building, facing the sea, a triangular balcony protruded like the prow of a ship, supported on huge metal brackets which curved in a graceful arc to the base of the wall. The house was arranged as a rectangle, with a courtyard in the centre out of which rose a circular stone tower. The tower was twice the height of the main building and appeared to have a room at the top, rather like an airport control tower, from which an observer would be able to look out in every direction. The Crow's Nest, thought Tom. But what really did the trick, what really made Shipley Manor appear to be sitting in the sea, was the sparkling blue moat which surrounded it.

It was a wonderful view, one which Tom might have enjoyed for longer. But being on time for his interview was far more important to him, so he continued on. The driveway took him to the rear of the house. There, a wooden drawbridge led over the moat to a pair of large oak doors. On either side of these doors stood a treadmill, each almost as tall as the building itself. Tom stopped to examine one of them. It was like a giant hamster wheel, suspended at its hub on ornate metal struts which protruded from the building, allowing it to spin free of the ground. Each side of the treadmill looked like a bicycle wheel, its rusty spokes leaving just enough room to squeeze through to the middle, where dozens of metre-wide planks had been placed to create an inner walkway. Tom could see that walking inside the wheel would make it turn. He could also see various cables and pulleys which led from the treadmills into the house, through two holes in the wall. He was considering what these might be for when a small hatch opened in one of the doors and a man's voice rang out.

'Ahoy there, young man, can I help you?'

Tom fumbled nervously in his pocket and pulled out the advert.

'I've come about the job advertised in the *Shipley Gazette*,' he replied.

'Ah, you must be Tom,' the voice boomed. 'Welcome aboard.'

Before he could reply, the door swung open and Tom stood facing a long dark corridor leading into the house. The owner of the voice was already several paces ahead of Tom and beckoning for him to follow.

As quick as he could, Tom closed the heavy door behind him and tried to catch up with the man without breaking the 'don't run in corridors' rule. Suddenly, the man turned left and disappeared through a doorway. Tom reached the doorway a few seconds later and peered inside. A puzzled frown crept across his face. The room was circular, with a domed ceiling painted with clouds and blue sky, from which hung several wooden seagulls on almost invisible wires. The floor, though flat, was painted to look like the sea, its rising and falling foam-tipped waves reflecting the painted blue sky above and the bright glimmer of sunlight flooding in through a round window in the wall. The sea extended half-way up the walls, where it met the sky to form a 360-degree horizon. In the centre of the room stood a raised platform, like a raft, made from lengths of old timber tied together with rope. On it stood two old barrels across which rested a flat piece of wood to make a desk. There were two chairs, one on Tom's side of the desk and one on the other side, in which sat the man with the voice.

'I'm the Captain – pleased to meet you,' he said. 'Come and sit down, but make sure you don't fall in, there are sharks in them there waters.'

Between the door and the platform were three half-barrels which Tom realised he was supposed to use as stepping stones. Although they looked like whole barrels floating half-submerged in real sea, Tom knew that they weren't, of course, so it came as a big surprise when he stepped on to the first one and it wobbled so much he nearly fell off. He kept his balance, though, and after leaning back to close the door behind him, he stepped across the other two barrels and on to the platform, which bucked and swayed for a few seconds when he landed. He lowered himself slowly into the chair, and told himself he wasn't going to get seasick.

Across the desk sat a jovial-looking man, a few years older than Tom's father. He had long black hair gathered into a dozen dreadlocks and a large black beard reaching down from his chin. His eyes were friendly, with little crow's feet in the corners, and his grin revealed a set of straight white teeth which looked slightly too big for his mouth. He was wearing a chequered apron beneath which appeared to be a naval officer's uniform, and on his head sat the tallest chef's hat Tom had ever seen.

'Welcome to the Captain's Cabin,' he said. 'Please excuse the outfit, I was in the middle of cooking. That's my main job round here. Captain Cook they call me sometimes.' He gave a hearty chuckle, and the raft wobbled precariously as he got up and walked round to Tom's side of the desk. He lowered himself to Tom's level as if he didn't wish to be overheard.

'Now look,' he said in a low voice, 'the tide will be in soon, so I'll get straight to the point – if you can answer this question, the job of cabin boy is yours.'

'I'll do my best,' Tom replied nervously.

'Very well then,' said the Captain, and he looked round again before continuing. 'Where in the Seven Seas are my reading glasses? I've been searching for them all day.'

Tom smiled with some relief, because he knew exactly where they were. He could see them.

'They're sticking out of your beard,' he said. 'Right next to the knife and fork.'

The Captain brought his hands up to his beard and prodded around with his fingers.

'Whereabouts in my beard?' he asked. 'Which country?'

'Sorry?' replied Tom, not understanding the question.

'Peru? Chile? Brazil?' answered the Captain.

It was then that Tom realised the Captain's beard was trimmed into the shape of South America. Tom didn't know a lot about South America, but he did know that Brazil was by far the largest country there, so he decided to take a guess.

'I think they're in Brazil,' he said. The Captain put his hands on them immediately.

'Sooo they are,' he bellowed, delighted to have found them. 'Well, I'll be a sea urchin's uncle, I must have put them there after reading the morning papers. I keep everything in my beard, you know – pens, cutlery, a light snack occasionally. Very convenient. And having a beard in the shape of South America is such a shipshape way of remembering where I've put things. Cutlery in Caracas, pens in Peru, bifocals in Brazil, you get the idea. The only problem, of course, is that sometimes I don't remember what things are called.'

'Anyway,' continued the Captain, getting back to business, 'a promise is a promise, and never let it be said that the Captain doesn't keep his promises. You are now the Shipley Manor cabin boy – congratulations,' and he held out his hand.

Tom shook it firmly.

'I'll ask Polly to give you a guided tour.' With that, the Captain reached round and picked up a length of black hose which was sticking out from the top of his desk like an elephant's trunk. He put his lips to the brass funnel attached to the end and blew a loud raspberry into it.

'I don't really have to do that, but I do so enjoy the sound,' he explained with a wink. Then he shouted into the funnel, 'This is the Captain speaking. Would Polly please come to the Captain's Cabin – we have a new crew member on board.' Finally he blew hard into the funnel, as if to help the words on their way. He turned to Tom. 'Brilliant system, don't you think? We call them blowpipes. Seymour rigged them up. Every room has a pipe leading to the loudspeakers on top of the Crow's Nest, so we can send messages to each other wherever we are in the house or grounds. You can even hear them down in the cellar. Have you met Seymour yet? Never mind, you will. Ah, here's Polly. Goodbye, young man.'

And he was gone.

Until now Tom had been wondering whether the strangest thing he'd encountered that day had been the talking sheep or the Captain's beard. But now he could see that top prize would have to go to the girl who had just appeared in the doorway.

Getting the Fizzle

Polly Seabright was much smaller than Tom, with huge brown eyes and a little upturned nose. Her most striking feature, though, was a pair of thick, jet-black eyebrows which all but joined in the middle and reached almost from ear to ear. Tom thought she looked about ten years old, which made her a couple of years younger than him. She was dressed from the neck down in a shimmering green and blue sequinned leotard which stretched tight over her body, arms and legs like a coating of fish scales. On her feet she wore a matching pair of delicate slip-on shoes. Her hair was naturally black but had been coloured bright gold and twisted into long strands which curled and rose up a full two gravity-defying feet above her head. Each strand was decorated with glittering starfish, seahorses and other colourful and exotic sea creatures. Finally, at her ankles the legs of the leotard flared out sideways, so that when she stood with her feet together she appeared to be standing on a large tailfin.

Today, Polly had decided to dress up as a mermaid.

Tom was lost for words.

'It's just a little something I threw on,' Polly said, having heard the expression somewhere before.

Still Tom didn't reply, so she skipped straight over the barrels and on to the platform to join him.

'They've got old car suspension springs holding them up,' she told him, pointing towards the wobbly barrels. 'Quite realistic, don't you think, especially the raft – it's got one big spring right in the middle so it wobbles really well.' To prove her point she hopped from one foot to the other, making the raft sway so much that Tom had to grip on to the desk to stop his chair from sliding into the sea. He stood up and faced her.

'My name's Tom,' he managed finally, holding out his hand politely. 'Pleased to meet you.'

From nowhere Polly pulled out a large red gobstopper and plonked it into Tom's hand.

'Shall we go?' she said.

Three skips later they were back in the corridor. Polly seemed happy to lead Tom round and tell him all about Shipley Manor. He in turn decided it would be polite to eat the gobstopper she had so generously given him, so the conversation was rather one-sided. The corridor was lined with portraits of the Captain's ancestors. As Polly introduced each of the paintings in turn, Tom learned that the Captain was in fact Lord Horatio Shipley, the latest in a long line of Lord and Lady Shipleys who had lived in the Manor for well over two hundred years. The Captain had left Shipley Manor to join the navy when he was sixteen, and had sailed round the world several times before becoming Captain of his own ship. The sea and ships were his passion. However, when his parents grew old he returned to take care of them, and promised he would look after the ancestral home after their death. True to his word, the Captain had stayed at Shipley Manor.

'But he was desperate to return to the sea really,' Polly said. 'He used to spend hours gazing down the valley towards the coast. Sometimes he would even forget to eat for days on end. Eventually, my mum says, he realised that if he was ever going to be happy at Shipley Manor there was something he had to do.'

Somehow, no matter what the cost, the Captain decided to make Shipley Manor feel like a ship. So although the main building remained the same, he set about replacing its square windows with portholes and building the enormous Crow's Nest, which Tom had rightly identified, up through the courtyard. On the roof, facing south towards the sea, he built a glass conservatory resembling a ship's bridge, in which he installed a large ship's wheel. From there he could pretend he was once again at the helm of a ship. Almost. There was still something missing – water. The Captain yearned to look straight down and see water lapping at the sides of the house. He wanted it so much, he spent every last penny he had on building a deep, wide moat around it.

'That's when he discovered Fizzle,' said Polly.

Tom, who hadn't said anything up to this point, recognised the word from the advert and took the gobstopper discreetly out of his mouth. He wrapped it in his handkerchief and put it carefully in his pocket.

'What's Fizzle?' he asked.

'Come on, I'll show you,' replied Polly, and she led him out of the corridor and into the central courtyard. The Crow's Nest, which was now in front of them, rose from the centre of a huge compass carved into the stone floor around its base. As well as the points of the compass there were numerous other lines pointing outwards, each marked with the name of a faraway destination and its distance in miles. Tom guessed, quite rightly, that these were some of the Captain's favourite places. He certainly liked his food.

Hank's Deli, New York, USA: 3,420

Mamma Mango's Beach Café, Kingston, Jamaica: 4,638

Bonza Tucker, Sydney, Australia: 10,588

Tom also noticed that a ramp, rather like a helter-skelter at a funfair, spiralled upwards from the base of the tower, finally joining a metal walkway which ran full circle around the room at the top.

Polly saw him gazing upwards.

'We can go up there later if you like, but I'll let Seymour show you round it properly, it's his room,' she said. 'I'm thirsty, let's go and get some Fizzle.'

Tom followed Polly across the courtyard and in through another door, above which was a sign saying 'Captain's Cocktail Lounge – Get the Fizzle'. They descended a flight of steep wooden steps into the room below. The room was quite dark, but there were two small portholes at the far end which were letting in some light. Tom looked more closely. There was something strange about them: they were sort of . . . blurry. Then he realised. They had gone below ground level, which meant they were also below the surface of the moat. Of course the view was blurry – he was looking straight into water.

Polly called Tom over from behind the heavy wooden bar and he slid on to a bar stool facing her. Looking around, Tom saw that the walls were decorated with several large tropical fish, each about a metre long and made from wood. Under each fish was written a name – 'Neon Rainbow Fish', 'Pink Kisser', 'Spotted Green Puffer Fish' – so Tom assumed that the bright colours and intricate patterns in which they were painted were authentic. In most cases the fish were beautiful and friendly-looking, but there were also a few really vicious-looking specimens, such as the African Tiger Fish. Tom was glad this particular one was only made from wood – it looked as though it could bite your arm off in one go. Small brass hinges attached the fishes' fins to their bodies, enabling them to flap freely. Tom was about to turn back to Polly when he saw what looked like a Spotted Green Puffer Fish float past the window outside. Its tail was moving from side to side, pushing it along. Tom nearly fell off his stool.

'We call them Fizzlefish,' explained Polly, as she grabbed his arm and helped him back on to his seat properly. 'All the little bubbles in the Fizzle make the wooden fins wiggle, so the fish swim around. It looks quite realistic, doesn't it? We usually have about twenty of them swimming in the moat, but sometimes we need to take them out to repaint them or oil their hinges. That's my job. I've got a long Fizzlestick, with a hook on the end, and each fish has a small ring on the top of its head. Sometimes it takes me hours to hook one out.' Polly handed Tom a menu. 'You're allowed anything.'

Tom examined the menu. The drinks had names like 'Sea Serpent Surprise', 'Shark Bite' and 'Walk the Plank', and each of them had Fizzle as its main ingredient. For example, a 'Fizzbang Dollop' was described as 'a whale-sized dollop of the Captain's finest rum-flavoured ice-cream floating in a sea of Magic Fizzle'. Tom thought that sounded a bit fancy. Perhaps it would be more sensible to go for something simple, so that he could taste the Fizzle better.

While he was choosing, Polly explained that when the Captain had decided to build the moat, he bought himself a second-hand mechanical digger to excavate it. The first time he had plunged the digger into the ground, a jet of water had shot hundreds of feet into the air. As it had rained back down, the Captain had tipped his head back to catch some in his mouth. It made his tongue tingle, so he collected a whole bucketful. And when he saw how clear it was, and how it was full of millions of fizzy bubbles dancing around, he couldn't resist drinking some more.

'What happened next?' asked Tom.

'We call it "Getting the Fizzle",' replied Polly. 'Try it for yourself.'

So Tom ordered an 'Iceberg Crunch'. Polly put a handful of crushed ice in the bottom of a tall glass, added a slice of lemon and filled it to the top with Fizzle, poured from a large blue bottle standing on the bar next to her. Tom peered out of the porthole again. Polly seemed to know what he was thinking.

'Don't worry,' she assured him. 'We don't drink it straight from the moat, we get it from the spring.'

She made another one for herself, but didn't put the top back on the bottle when she'd finished.

'That's the other thing about it,' she told Tom, catching his glance. 'It never ever loses its fizz, even when you leave the top off. It's magic, you see.'

Tom didn't believe that for one minute, of course, but he lowered himself down for a closer look anyway, until his nose was almost touching the glass. It looked like ordinary mineral water to him. Lots of bouncing bubbles all right, but he'd seen that before. Magic indeed! Maybe the Captain had slammed the digger into an ordinary water main.

'Well, are you going to drink it or look at it?' Polly challenged him with a grin. 'Scared?'

'No,' said Tom indignantly and took a large gulp. Nothing happened, although he had to admit it was strangely tasty.

'So have you "Got the Fizzle" yet?' asked Polly eagerly.

'Nope, I don't think so,' said Tom and he took another gulp. Still nothing. Then a third.

'Of course, you have to believe in magic for it to work,' explained Polly. 'You *do* believe in magic, don't you?'

Tom shook his head firmly. Of course he didn't believe in such foolishness. But he answered politely.

'No, I don't – sorry.'

'Well,' said Polly, sounding slightly disappointed, 'you will after you've worked here for a while. Then you'll "Get the Fizzle" for sure. Come on, let's go.'

Tom finished off his drink and followed Polly back upstairs to the courtyard. She led him to the base of the Crow's Nest. Tom looked up at the circular glass room which sat right at the top. It looked deserted.

'Come on,' said Polly, and before Tom had a chance to reply she had started running up the ramp. A quarter of the way up she leaned over the edge and shouted to Tom to follow, which he did, if a little reluctantly – surely slides were for sliding DOWN, rather than climbing UP? He was quite a fit boy, having spent years going on early morning runs with his father, so he made good progress. But he was surprised to find that he wasn't catching up with Polly – she ended up waiting for him on the walkway at the top.

From there Tom could see right down the valley to the sea, but he could also see glimpses of the road at the top of the woods, and various outbuildings and greenhouses among the trees. In fact, he could see just about everything from the walkway, including the gap in the fence where the sheep had spoken to him – or rather hadn't spoken to him, because he knew full well that sheep couldn't talk. Best of all, though, he now had a really good view of the magnificent gardens stretching out in front of Shipley Manor. The main lawn was also 'shipshape', tapering to a long, elegant point like the deck of a luxury liner. Then it fell away down steep banks to rougher ground below where during the winter, according to Polly, thousands of snowdrops bloomed like frothy white bow-waves. To the right of the house stood a row of seaside beach huts which were used as changing rooms by visitors who wished to swim in the moat. They were painted in a variety of coloured spots, stripes and zigzags, so that each one looked completely different.

'So you don't walk into the wrong one by mistake,' explained Polly.

And to the left Tom could see a separate area of lawn, with its own picnic tables, behind which stood six small log cabins. These, he presumed, were to be his main responsibility.

'Magic, isn't it?' said Polly. Tom groaned inside. He knew that Polly probably just meant the view was beautiful – he thought so too, so why call it something it clearly wasn't? That was just silly. As he was thinking of a reply that didn't sound too rude, Polly peered over the edge of the walkway and announced that Seymour had arrived and was waiting for them at the bottom.

'Coming down,' she yelled, and straightaway launched herself down the ramp on her back. In an instant she had disappeared around the first bend.

Tom hesitated for a moment, then sat down to follow her. The ride down was breathtaking. The surface of the ramp was so smooth that he almost flew down, the wind in his face, occasionally catching a glimpse of Polly's streaming hair as she hurtled round the bend in front of him. When Tom reached the bottom, a large mat brought him to a sudden halt. He sat there for a moment, almost laughing. That was fan-tastic. Normally, he would have been worried sick about getting his trousers dirty, but as the slide was the only way down, he couldn't possibly have broken any rules, could he? He saw Polly smile at him, as if somehow she'd caught him out. He jumped up and dusted himself off. Polly stood facing him, with one hand resting on the back of a wheelchair. Seymour Boff was sitting in it stroking a fluffy white cat which was settled on his lap. All eyes were on Tom.

'Hello, young man,' said the cat.

Eau d'Executive

Tom and his father stood side by side at the kitchen sink. Roger was washing the dishes, checking each item against the light before handing it to Tom, who was in charge of drying. Tom had made his own way home from Shipley Manor – a walk to the main road, then a bus – in time for Sunday tea, which they had just finished eating together. During tea Tom told his father what had happened that afternoon. At first Roger thought Shipley Manor sounded rather odd, but when Tom explained that the owner was not only a real Lord but a former Captain in the navy, his attitude changed to one of approval.

'It sounds just the job, Tom,' he had nodded. 'Plenty of naval discipline, some good hard work in a healthy environment and earning your own money at the same time – what could be better?'

Tom thought it best not to mention his encounters with talking animals. He was still no nearer an explanation for that, and even though Polly and Seymour must have heard the cat speak, neither of them had batted an eyelid. So he'd ignored it too, even though he'd found it very unsettling. Perhaps he should mention it to Polly on his next visit.

After the cat incident, Seymour had promised to show Tom his workshop the following week and Polly had taken Tom to see the cabins. There were six in all. During the winter they were empty, but when the weather warmed up paying guests would stay there. Polly said they came to 'Get the Fizzle'. Their main use, though, was at the peak of the summer holidays, when children from the city were allowed to stay there for free. During their week's stay they would be able to swim in the moat, explore the woods, play games and enjoy all kinds of entertainment. But they also had lessons from some of the live-in staff. Maggie Seabright, Polly's mother, ran art classes (the tropical fish in the Captain's Cocktail Lounge had all been decorated by visiting children), the Captain taught the children how to cook and let them help in the kitchen, and Seymour ran science workshops in the Crow's Nest, where they would invent and build things. And if they had any energy left over at the end of the day, they could run around inside one of the treadmills for half an hour. The treadmills were attached to a generator inside the house which stored the energy made by each turn of the wheel and converted it into electricity. A good half-hour workout inside one of the tread-mills would generate enough power to light the house for a day, or heat enough water for five baths, or cook lunch. All the electricity in Shipley Manor was generated in this way, and the treadmills were nearly always in use. After all, who wants to sit in a cold bath?

In fact, Shipley Manor was almost self-sufficient. It had its own water and electricity supplies and the residents grew enough food in the vegetable patches and greenhouses to last throughout the year. Besides that, there were chickens for laying eggs, beehives for honey, a cow which provided plenty of milk and cheese, and several sheep, which were shorn once a year to provide enough wool for Maggie to knit a couple of outfits for Polly. And because they were all happy to get by on the small amount of money they earned from renting out the cabins and selling the odd bottle of Fizzle to their guests, they never had enough to go on shopping trips. It was no wonder that Shipley Manor was little known in the town. Apart from the occasional trip to the market, its residents rarely set foot there.

Tom's weekend job would be to keep the cabins clean and ensure that every visitor had new bedding and bathroom linen, and a complimentary bottle of Fizzle by the bed when they arrived. And if there were no visitors arriving that weekend, the Captain would find him some other way to earn his wages, like helping out in the kitchen or gardens. Apart from that, he could come and go as he pleased and use all the facilities, so long as he didn't mind mucking in if something needed doing.

He was to start his new job next weekend.

The following morning Roger dropped Tom off at the school gates and continued into work. With a little stab of embarrassment he parked his old second-hand car in the only space left, next to the expensive new sports car which belonged to his colleague Barclay Grub.

If you saw Roger Sterling and Barclay Grub side by side, you might be tempted – quite rightly in this case – to judge Roger to be the smarter, more honest and more hardworking of the two. He was tall, well-built and smartly dressed. His short dark hair was always neatly trimmed and he had an open, sincere face and a friendly smile. Most of all, he looked you in the eye when he talked to you. Barclay Grub, on the other hand, was none of these things. He was a short, squat man. His hair reached down past his collar at the back and a few wispy strands stretched from just above his left ear all the way over his head in a failed attempt to conceal the baldness on top. Dandruff speckled the shoulders of his unwashed pin-stripe suit and a thin moustache extended an inch in each direction above his rather wet, rubbery lips. Instead of washing, he kept his pockets full of free after-shave sachets, which he scavenged daily from chemists' shops in Shipley High Street. He would open several of these a day – his favourite was 'Eau d'Executive' – so that he could slap a fresh handful of pungent liquid around his face, to disguise the smell of his unwashed body. But the worst things about Barclay Grub were the things you couldn't see at first glance, the things he tried to keep hidden, so that even people who worked with him every day, like Tom's father, weren't fully aware of them. His treachery. His dishonesty. His mean-ness. And his greed. Roger was no fool, but he was blind to how bad Grub really was. He kept telling himself, as he told Tom, that it was wrong to judge people by their appearance alone. Besides, Grub was manager of the bank, a position of authority which, as a rule, automatically commanded Roger's loyalty and respect. For these reasons he tended to overcompensate for Grub, constantly looking for his good points and finding excuses for the bad ones. Today, for example, there was a note waiting for him on his desk. It said: 'See me immediately. Grub.' Now Roger would have written something more like 'Roger – a quick word please. Barclay,' but by the time he'd reached Grub's office door, Roger had convinced himself that it wasn't a rude message at all. Barclay Grub was a very busy man, in charge of Roger and a dozen other employees. He simply didn't have time to write polite, friendly messages.

Roger knocked three times.

'Come,' shouted a voice from inside. Roger entered and walked up to Barclay Grub's desk.

'Good morning, Mr Grub,' he said cheerfully.

Grub ignored him and continued prodding away at his calculator, whilst simultaneously reaching out with his free hand to thrust a piece of paper towards Roger. Roger picked it up and looked at it.

'What do you call that, Sterling?' demanded Grub. Roger recognised it at once.

'It's the loan contract you asked me to draw up for that engineering company – I left it on your desk last night.'

Grub carried on tapping at his calculator.

'Why, is there something wrong with it?' continued Roger.

There was a long pause. Finally, with one hard, emphatic stab of the Equals button, Barclay Grub leaned back in his fake-leather chair and looked up at Roger. With a short wave of his hand he beckoned Roger to return the piece of paper to him, which he did.

'I'll tell you what's wrong with it, Sterling,' he sighed, holding the document up like an exhibit in a murder trial. 'You can read it, that's what's wrong with it.'

'But isn't that the idea?' replied Roger defensively.

'You know damned well it's not, Sterling,' Grub barked back. 'If customers were meant to read small print, they would all be born with magnifying glasses in front of their eyes. Now I'd like it redrafted – but this time think small. Think "fitting-the-telephone-director-on-the-back-of-a-postage-stamp", think "the-Bible-printed-on-the-head-of-a pin", think "ten-thousand-reasons-why-Roger-Sterling-never-made-it-past-bank-clerk" written on the top of this calculator button here. Am I making myself clear, Sterling?'

Roger didn't move. He certainly wasn't about to question his boss, but at the same time he couldn't help thinking that it was wrong to deliberately print the type so small that no one could read it, and that made him feel very uncomfortable indeed.

Barclay Grub knew this, and with another deep sigh he tried a different tack.

'Look at it this way, Sterling. The smaller the type on our loan contracts the less paper we use, the less paper we use the fewer trees we need to chop down. Imagine if all the banks in the country did this. We'd save whole forests. We need to set an example, don't we, Sterling? We need to show that the environment comes first. That we care.'

The trick worked. Now that Roger could see a positive side to what he was being asked to do, he readily agreed.

In any case, he could hardly afford to lose his job; he had his beloved son Tom to look after. Which reminded him.

'There is one other thing, Mr Grub,' he said. 'I was wondering whether I might be able to do some extra work on Saturdays. My son starts a Saturday job at a country house called Shipley Manor next week, so I'm free to come in if you need me. The extra money would be really useful.'

Barclay seemed interested.

'Shipley Manor, you say. I've never heard of it – tell me more . . .'

Roger was pleasantly surprised at Grub's interest in his son's Saturday job. So he told him as much as he knew about Shipley Manor: about how beautiful the estate was, the holiday cabins, and how it had its own spring water which the residents thought had magical powers, no doubt because it possessed some kind of restorative, health-giving properties. Finally, he explained how the 'eccentric' owner had spent the last of the family wealth making the house 'shipshape' and building the moat. And the more he described it, the more upright Grub sat, the more alert he became, like a hyena sniffing fresh prey. Soon, he was positively fidgeting with excitement.

'It sounds like a potential gold-mine to me, but Tom says they've got no real interest in making huge amounts of money,' Roger concluded.

But *I* have, thought Grub, as he drew the meeting to a close. 'I'll let you know about Saturdays, thank you, Roger,' he said out loud.

As Roger turned his back to leave the room, Grub shot him a contemptuous glance.

'Show me an honest man and I'll show you a loser,' he mumbled to himself as he reached for the phone.

A Secret Meeting

In the office of the Chief Executive of Shipley Town Council, a computer was coming under attack.

'You pathetic, pus-filled pile of putrescent picabytes!'

A bony fist hammered down on the top of the computer monitor.

'Do You Want To Quit?' asked the computer.

'No, of course I don't want to quit, you disgusting, dim-witted diode-brain.'

The fist came down again.

'Do You Want To Quit?' repeated the computer.

The Chief Executive hammered the top of the monitor once more, then bent down and yanked the plug out of the wall. She held it up to the blank screen. 'Who's the boss now then, eh? The next time I tell you to print something, just do it, you glorified typewriter!'

She threw the plug on to the floor. 'Computers!' she spat. 'Give me a row of secretaries any day – at least when they get something wrong you can ssssack them.'

Venetia Pike reclined in her red leather executive chair and tried to compose herself by admiring her newly decorated office. 'No expense spared,' she purred. 'Tasteful . . . yet modern.' The room's colour scheme was predominantly pink. The floor was covered in a bright pink carpet, thick enough to wiggle your toes in, with the walls painted in a matching but much lighter shade. Facing her desk a luxurious pink sofa sat next to a small side table on which were placed several magazines and news-papers. The *Shipley Gazette* rested on top of the pile, but if you explored underneath you would have found several other titles including *Fashion Weekly*, *Cosmetic Surgery Today* and perhaps most curiously, *Reptile World*. Or perhaps not that curiously, if you knew what Venetia Pike kept in her attic at home.

The phone rang. It was Barclay Grub.

'How's my fluffy bunny today?' he cooed. Pike lifted her eyes to the ceiling and took a deep breath. That malodorous little man made her skin crawl, but he was useful to her.

'Your fluffy bunny's very upset,' she replied in a girly voice. 'Her cuddly-wuddly grubby man hasn't been to see her for aaaaages.'

'Tomorrow, my little plum pudding,' he replied. 'I've something very interesting to tell you. I think we may have hit the jackpot.'

'Sounds fascinating, darling,' she replied. 'Come at twelve, I'll make sure we're not disturbed.' And she put the phone down. 'Creep,' she muttered under her breath.

At noon the next day, Barclay Grub stopped outside the Council offices and slapped a handful of 'Eau d'Executive' over his face before entering the building. He rode the lift to the top floor, licking the palms of his hands and smoothing strands of wind-blown hair back into position across the top of his head. He brushed some of the dandruff from his shoulders – most of which stuck to his clammy hands – and managed to take one last look in the mirror before the lift went 'Ping' and spat him out on to Pike's floor.

Venetia Pike was waiting for him in the doorway of her office.

'Barclay, daaarling, how lovely to see you.'

Grub waddled down the corridor towards her, barely able to stop himself from breaking into a run.

She was magnificent – from the top of her white-blonde head to the toes of her red stilettos, from the ends of her impossibly long eyelashes to the tips of her inch-long fingernails – she was just . . . *magnificent*. Grub reached the door and Pike moved to one side to let him into the room. She followed him in, closed the door quietly behind her and offered up a hand for him to kiss. He kissed it greedily several times before she withdrew it and sat down on the sofa. She patted the space next to her.

'Shall we make ourselves comfortable?' she said. Grub sat down and balanced his briefcase on his knees.

'This is it, Venetia,' he panted. 'I've found the perfect place for us. If we can get our hands on it, we'll make a fortune.'

He told Pike what he'd heard about the extraordinary house, the extensive grounds and the natural spring water. She smiled when he said that some people believed the water had magical powers.

Wonderful, she thought. The more people believe in that rubbish, the more we'll be able to bottle it up and sell it to them.

'The place is run,' continued Grub, 'by someone who spends his entire time pretending it's a ship and letting young tearaways from the city stay there for free. He's got no business sense whatsoever, by the sound of it. Seems he just about scrapes by renting out one or two log cabins in the grounds. That's when he's not letting hordes of kids stay there for nothing, of course. I doubt if he even knows how much the place is worth, let alone how much money he could make if he turned it into a luxury hotel or built a housing estate on the land. And the best bit, my dearest, darling sweet pea,' he concluded, rubbing his hands together with excitement, 'is that he's flat broke. Would you believe it, the idiot spent every last penny he had building a moat – a *moat* – so that he could pretend to be at sea?'

This all sounded very interesting to Pike. Grub took her hand and continued.

'If we can pull this one off, we'll be rich enough to go away together and never have to work again.'

Pike resisted the temptation to pull her hand away. You mean I'll be rich enough to dump you for good, she thought.

They began planning their strategy. They had worked together like this before. It was all so simple. First, they would find someone who was in financial difficulty. That was easy for Grub – as manager of Shipley Bank, all he had to do was sneak a look at his customers' accounts on the computer to see how well they were doing. Once he'd found a suitable victim, perhaps a local farmer whose crops had failed, Pike would send in her Chief Council Inspector, Mr Tutt.

Now Mr Tutt wasn't part of the plot. He was probably the most incorruptible person in Shipley, but he was also the most thorough and, like Tom's father, a great believer in the saying 'rules are rules'. With a brain like an encyclopaedia, Mr Tutt knew every single Council by-law, regulation and directive going back hundreds of years. No one could get away with anything when Mr Tutt came to call. He'd find any breach of health and safety regulations, or planning and building law, and whatever was wrong with that unfortunate victim's premises, he would have to fix it. The penniless farmer might be told to buy an expensive new combine harvester because the old one was unsafe, or spend a fortune putting new roofs on his barns to make them fireproof. Somehow, he would have to find the money. Because if he didn't fix all the faults Mr Tutt found, Pike would send an official letter from the Council ordering the farm to be closed down. He'd be out of business.

And that's when Barclay Grub's sweaty, smiling face would appear at his victim's door. Pretending he had come to the rescue like a knight in shining armour, he would brandish one of his specially drawn-up loan contracts, and offer to lend the unsuspecting victim the money he needed. A new combine harvester? No problem, sir, Shipley Bank is here to help, just sign on the dotted line and the money to buy it is yours. But, as the farmer and many others discovered, as soon as they'd spent every penny meeting Mr Tutt's Council standards, Grub would return. But this time he wouldn't be smiling. And neither would the thick-necked bailiffs he would take along whenever he knew that his victim was bigger than he was. There and then he would demand *all* the money back. No time to save, or wait for next year's harvest. Pay up in full, within the hour, or the bank will seize your property, and you'll be left without so much as a grain of corn. By Law. Naturally, most of his victims thought that this couldn't possibly be true. Surely they could pay the money back little by little every month, like any normal loan. But then Grub would draw their attention to the microscopic small print in the contract they'd signed eagerly just a few weeks before. It was his favourite moment, like a boxer delivering a knock-out punch. He just loved watching the blood drain from his victims' faces when they read it. When they knew they'd been caught like a fly in a spider's web, with no possibility of escape.

Or . . . so they would think.

Because then the unfortunate victim would receive a mysterious phone call from the Shipley

Property Investment Company, which just happened to be owned by Venetia Pike and Barclay Grub. It would offer to buy their property for a fraction of its real value, just enough for them to repay the bank loan and have a small amount left over. Most people had no choice but to agree and, so far, Pike and Grub had bought six properties in this way, each time selling them for a vast profit just a few months later. But they had never gone after anything as big as Shipley Manor before. If they could pull it off it would be the bargain of the century.

'How did you find out about the place?' Pike asked Grub.

'From one of my idiot staff,' Grub replied. 'His son has just started working there.'

'Well, keep him ssssweet, darling,' advised Pike. 'He might come in useful.'

After Pike had managed to ease Grub out of the door, she went to her desk and took out a canister of 'Essence of Ozone' air freshener. She sprayed it liberally around the room and gave an extra-long burst over Grub's end of the sofa. Then she went back to her desk and picked up her phone.

'Good morning, Mr Tutt. It seems there is a property which has escaped the Council's attention for far too long.'

The Captain's Table

Some years earlier, Shipley Manor had been at the centre of a Great Storm. The estate had suffered the storm's full fury and during that night almost a quarter of its trees were uprooted and blown over, or smashed in half at the trunk, leaving jagged wooden spikes sticking out of the earth like huge crooked fingers.

The following day Slugbucket the gardener – whom Tom had yet to meet – and the Captain ventured sadly into the woods to inspect the damage and decide what was to be done. After much chin-rubbing, they came up with the idea of using the broken and fallen tree-trunks to create an adventure playground, set along a winding woodland trail. Parents, they reasoned, would enjoy walking through the woods whilst their children played on the different wooden apparatus encountered along the way. Result: happy children, happy mums and dads and plenty of hungry and thirsty customers for the Captain's Cocktail Lounge. Yes, that's what they would do.

So Slugbucket began what turned out to be several years of hard work sawing, carving and building. Some of the fallen tree-trunks he carved into giant water snakes or sea lizards which you could climb on. Those broken tree-trunks which had been left standing were carved into all kinds of sea creatures, some fearsome, like fire-breathing sea dragons, and some more friendly, like noble seahorses and playful dolphins. And when Slugbucket ran out of animals to carve, he started making tree monsters with hideous gnarled faces and huge clawing hands that would tap you on the shoulder . . . if you forgot to duck at the right time.

The rest of Shipley Manor had been busy too. Polly's mum filled the lower branches with wind chimes assembled from coloured glass, fragments of broken mirror, milk-bottle tops and anything else which would tinkle in the breeze. On sunny days these would reflect swarms of light-spots on to the house, which would dart around in time with the breeze like a shoal of luminous goldfish. Higher up in the trees, the Captain suspended hundreds of hollow tubes cut from old drainpipes, so that when the wind blew across their hollow ends they hooted in harmony, like a choir of owls. It was a wonderful place by day, but at night, when the adventure trail was closed, the wood could become a very frightening place to be in, especially if you lost your way. It became known as Beastlybark Wood.

Polly wasn't scared of it, though. She knew every inch of the wood and had given Slugbucket many of the ideas for it. One of her favourites was the giant octopus which Slugbucket fashioned from the twisted roots of an enormous upturned oak tree. Positioned next to the moat, its tentacles waved and curled high into the air, stretching far enough over the water to be used as diving boards. But best of all was the secret platform that Slugbucket built for Polly as a special thank you for all her help. Hidden in an evergreen tree just above the entrance to the trail, it was called Polly's Perch, and standing on it she was able to see the house and the entire valley stretching beyond.

It was from here that Polly could now see Tom approaching. It was his first day, and he'd spent the morning cleaning bathrooms in the cabins. It had been hard work but he'd enjoyed it. He liked things to be clean. Polly jumped down and ran over to greet him. She was dressed from head to foot in yellow, with black stripes running down the sides of her arms and legs. Tom couldn't help smiling.

A banana today, he concluded.

'We're having a special lunchtime meeting,' she said excitedly. 'You're invited too – come on.'

She led Tom into the house and up the main staircase to the top floor. There, a spiral staircase took them up and out through a small doorway on to the roof, delivering them a few yards from the conservatory. Through the glass Tom could see several people milling around and, at the far end of the room, the ship's wheel just as Polly had described it, looking down the valley to the sea beyond. Everyone hushed as they went inside.

'Welcome, Tom,' boomed a voice. It was the Captain. He strode over to Tom and put his arm around him, much to Tom's embarrassment. 'Shipmates,' he announced to everyone, 'this is our new cabin boy. His name is Tom and I hope that we shall all get to know him over lunch. But first things first – food!'

The Captain thrust a plate into Tom's hand and Polly nudged him towards a large round table. It was full of interesting dishes, none of which Tom recognised. Polly explained that on board a real ship, honoured guests would regularly be invited to dine with the Captain, at the 'Captain's Table', where they could sample food from whichever part of the world they were in. The Captain liked to keep this seafaring tradition alive at Shipley Manor, so every so often he would pick a country and treat everyone to a local feast. Sometimes the food would be quite well-known. If it was Italy's turn, for example, there would be plenty of traditional pizzas as well as dishes like macaroni and spaghetti. But if the Captain chose Thailand, you could find yourself eating something more like fried scorpion or roasted water beetle.

'Of course, the Captain has to use ingredients from the garden or Shipley market, so we hardly ever get to try things like that.'

Tom wasn't sure that was such a bad thing.

Today it was Jamaica.

'Jamaica's good,' Polly reassured him.

They sat down at the table together. Polly piled her plate high straightaway, but Tom was more cautious. Perhaps it would be sensible to try things one at a time. He thought the banana fritters looked good, so he took one of those and poured himself a Pineapple Fizzle. A slim, rather nervous-looking woman with a permanently startled expression sat down next to him and introduced herself.

'I'm Edna Boff, Seymour's wife. Pleased to meet you, dear,' she said, holding out a frail, slightly jittery hand for Tom to shake, which he did.

'Pleased to meet you too,' replied Tom politely, before taking a bite of his fritter. Polly caught Tom glancing at Edna's hair. It was grey and stood on end as if she'd just been electrocuted.

'She's just been electrocuted,' Polly whispered. 'Seymour tries out all his inventions on her. She's had more electric shocks from his experiments than you've had hot dinners. Her hair sticks up like that all the time now.'

'Polly's right, dear,' said Edna, having heard every word. 'Yesterday I was trying out Seymour's new machine for washing, cutting and blow-drying hair all in one go. I should have refused, I suppose, but Seymour gets so enthusiastic about things it's difficult to say no.'

Suddenly, Tom was alarmed to feel a giggle bubbling up in his throat. What would his new employers think of him if he laughed at their misfortunes and sprayed them with half-eaten banana at the same time? Luckily for him, Edna continued talking and the moment passed.

'Now let's see, who don't you know?'

She went round the table clockwise, introducing him to the other diners. After Polly and Seymour sat an elderly, silver-haired woman. This was Seymour's mother, Constance Boff, who had recently moved into an apartment on the ground floor so that Seymour could look after her. Next to her was Slugbucket, the gardener. He was a very tall, strong-looking man with stooped shoulders and a long stubbly chin. Two huge hands poked out from his tatty brown jacket and these were busy feeding scraps of food to the fluffy white cat which was curling itself in and out of the legs of his chair.

'Why is he called Slugbucket?' Tom asked quietly.

'It's very simple,' replied Edna. 'Because every day he walks around the garden collecting slugs in a huge orange bucket. They eat the vegetables, you see, but he can't bear to kill them – or anything else for that matter – so he keeps them in a deep pit the size of a large paddling pool at the top of the woods, just above the vegetable patch. It's called the slug pit. He keeps them fed and watered and lets them live out their lives. And when they die they sink to the bottom and rot.'

'Doesn't the slug pit overflow?' asked Tom.

'Ah well, that's where Seymour does have his uses, you see. He invented a whole drainage system which leads out from the bottom of the slug pit and drains the liquid back into the soil. All the nutrients go into the vegetable patch or down into the orchard. He calls it his "Organic Soil Stimulant System". I call it "dead-slug juice" myself, but either way you wouldn't believe how big the fruit and vegetables grow here. Peas the size of Brussels sprouts, Brussels sprouts the size of tomatoes, tomatoes the size of grapefruits. And that, by the way, is Nautipus, the ship's cat,' Edna added, gesturing towards it.

'We've already met,' said Tom.

'Nautipus said hello to Tom last week,' explained Polly with a wicked grin. So she *had* heard.

'You and Seymour – what a pair!' Edna said, looking at Tom's expression then winking at Polly.

'Don't worry, Tom,' she continued in a hushed voice, 'most of the animals around here talk. It's perfectly normal – you'll find out soon enough.'

But Tom *did* worry, because there was nothing at all *normal* about it. Animals could *not* talk, and he wasn't about to start believing that they could. There had to be a proper explanation for what had happened. But as he couldn't think what it was yet, he leaned forward to pour himself another Pineapple Fizzle (which still had no effect on him, by the way), and when he sat back Edna continued with the introductions. On the other side of Slugbucket sat the Captain. He was talking to a very brightly dressed woman who turned out to be Polly's mother, Maggie Seabright. Maggie was a nurse who had come to Shipley Manor to look after Lord and Lady Shipley. She was also such a talented artist that when his parents died, the

Captain asked her to stay on to run art classes for the young summer visitors, and to be on hand in case any of them fell ill or, Heaven forbid, had an accident.

Tom realised that in fact, apart from old Constance, everyone round the table had lived at Shipley Manor for many years, having worked for Lord and Lady Shipley long before the Captain returned from sea. Maggie had been their nurse, Slugbucket their gardener, Edna the housekeeper and Seymour the general handyman. The last person at the table was sitting in a high chair between Maggie and Edna. She was about six months old, with a headful of short, spiky black hair, and was currently waving a wooden spoon full of Jamaican cornmeal porridge in the air. A large dollop splattered down on Tom's clean shirt. He recoiled as if he'd been shot. Aaaargh!

'You're honoured, Tom,' Maggie joked from the other side of the table. 'She only throws food at people she likes.'

Tom smiled back weakly, and began dabbing away at the stain with his handkerchief.

I'll explain that to Dad, he thought. He *will* be pleased.

'That's my new baby sister,' Polly explained proudly. 'Calypso – Mum and the Captain let me choose her name.'

This prompted one last question from Tom. He could see the Captain getting to his feet to speak, so he whispered it to Polly quickly: 'Does that mean the Captain is your father?'

She put her lips right up to his ear and whispered back.

'Yes,' she replied, 'but not my real one. He ran off when I was a baby. The Captain's better, though.'

On the other side of the table the Captain tapped a bottle of Fizzle with the end of his spoon.

'Shipmates,' he began, 'we have received a letter from Shipley Town Council which I would like to read to you.'

He reached into his beard and took out his reading glasses. Then, with a little cough to clear his throat, he began.

An Inspector Calls

To whom it may concern . . .

Under Rule 314 of the Business Premises Act
1925 (subsection 2) Shipley Manor is given notice
of a full and thorough Council Inspection, pursuant
to all conditions pertaining to its business
operations with particular reference to the 1948
Health and Safety at Work Act, the 1973 Food and
Drink Act, the 1963 Building and Planning
Regulations Act and Shipley Council By-Laws
Numbers 5, 11, 13 and 24 (subsection 6). Our
Chief Council Inspector Mr Leonard Tutt will arrive
to inspect the premises next Monday at 9.00am.
Your full co-operation would be appreciated.

By order of Shipley Town Council

'Oh lummy,' said Edna.

'Now, I've no idea what any of that lot actually means,' concluded the Captain grimly, 'but it sounds to me like we'd better make Mr Tutt feel at home when he arrives on Monday, and in the meantime get Shipley Manor looking as shipshape as possible. Oh, and one more thing – could everyone please do half an hour in the treadmills to get the generator topped up? The last thing we want is for the lights to go out when Mr Tutt is half-way down the cellar steps. Well, at least I *think* that's the last thing we want. Anyway, are we all agreed?'

Everyone appeared to be happy with the Captain's plan, and ten minutes later they all knew what they were going to do. Tom was to help Polly and Slugbucket in the garden once he'd finished cleaning the cabins. Edna would polish and clean the house and Seymour would spin round in his wheelchair, tidying away junk and touching up any chipped paintwork. The Captain would clean the kitchen and Maggie would look after Constance and keep everyone else supplied with snacks and fresh cups of tea, or Fizzle cocktails if they preferred.

But first Tom had an appointment with Seymour in the Crow's Nest, and as soon as the Captain's meeting was over Polly led him back into the courtyard and up the helter-skelter to the room at the top. Before Tom could say, 'Shouldn't we knock?' Polly had opened the door and stepped inside. Tom followed and looked around. In the centre of the room a white column stretched from floor to ceiling. The column ran right up through the centre of the building like a giant backbone, carrying blowpipes from every room in the house and connecting them to the four loudspeakers on the roof. A single waist-high work bench ran around the circumference of the room, its surface littered with technical drawings, ideas scribbled on scraps of paper and assorted toolkits. These in turn competed for space with half-built inventions bulging with cogs and pulleys, and the remains of dead computers, their insides scavenged for usable bits of electronic circuitry. And amongst this mess sat Seymour Boff, in front of something which looked like an electric keyboard, but with dozens of extra buttons and a microphone attached to the top. He'd arrived before them and was already wearing his special work hat. Two flexible stalks protruded from it like ant antennae – one with a spotlight at the end, the other with a magnifying glass. Seymour had designed it so that he could keep both hands free when he was working. Right now, though, his hands were busy pointing a telescope towards the top of the driveway, unaware that he himself was being watched. Tom was about to announce their arrival when Seymour leaned forward and spoke into the microphone.

'Hello, young man,' he said.

There was something about the way he said it that seemed familiar to Tom, something which gave him that hot prickly feeling up his back again. And then he realised.

'You're the sheep,' he cried.

Seymour nearly jumped out of his chair, but then he swivelled round with a huge grin on his face and held up his hands in surrender.

'And the cat,' he confessed.

'And the chickens,' added Polly, dancing gleefully from foot to foot.

So he'd been right all along: there *was* some perfectly simple explanation for the talking sheep. No magic required – what a relief. Polly and Seymour had obviously played a practical joke on him, just as Edna had implied. But before he could ask how it was done, Seymour beckoned him over to the window and handed him the telescope.

'You know the box at the top of the driveway, where our newspapers and post get dropped? Take a look.'

Tom aimed the telescope through the gap in the trees and focused it on the box. A postman was walking towards it carrying the second post. As he dropped it into the box, Seymour once again bent down to the microphone.

'Hello, young man.'

Straightaway the postman looked up and gave them a cheery wave, and had Tom been able to look closer he would also have seen him say, 'Hi, Seymour.'

So that was it, thought Tom.

'I've installed hidden speakers all over the estate,' Seymour explained. 'There's one by the post-box and one in the weeping willow tree at the bottom of the driveway, but most of them are close to where the animals feed – like the corner of the chicken run, and the fence by the water trough where you met the sheep last week. The children love it, especially the younger ones. I mean, real talking animals. As far as they're concerned, it's magic, and we certainly don't go out of our way to spoil the secret. You wouldn't believe some of the conversations I've had. Down by the chicken coop last year, one five-year-old asked me if I could lay her an Easter egg.'

But that didn't explain the talking cat.

'Oh, there's no great mystery there,' explained Seymour, smiling. 'I've spent the last ten years entertaining the children who come here during their summer holidays. I read stories to them, do card tricks, juggle, that kind of thing. But the main part of my act is ventriloquism. I've got a bit of a talent for it.'

This last sentence he said without moving his lips, just to illustrate the point.

'And just as I was starting to believe this place was full of magic,' Tom said jokingly.

Polly and Seymour glanced at each other.

'Oh, there's real magic here all right,' said Seymour quite seriously. 'The genuine thing. The place is literally dripping with it.'

Yeah right, thought Tom.

On his way back to the cabins, Tom passed the weeping willow tree. He felt lighter, as if a huge weight had been lifted from his shoulders, and now that he knew everything was normal and proper and right again, he couldn't resist trying a little experiment.

'Good afternoon,' he said to the tree as he walked past.

'It might be good for you, young man,' the tree wept miserably, 'but then I don't suppose a tree surgeon has just lopped off two of your favourite branches, has he?'

'Er – no,' replied Tom, grinning.

'There you go then,' sniffed the tree. 'Any chance of a hug?'

Tom laughed. 'Sorry,' he said. 'I've already got my shirt dirty once today.'

The tree burst out crying, and Tom continued on to the cabins.

Mr Tutt and his passenger, Venetia Pike, arrived at the gates of Shipley Manor right on time. Pike rarely accompanied Mr Tutt on his inspections, but on this occasion she wanted to see the place for herself. At first sight it looked promising. The imposing entrance clearly belonged to a substantial property, and she felt a hot flush of excitement as she realised that, for once, Grub may have been right about something. She stepped out of Mr Tutt's Council inspection van and gave the locked gates an impatient rattle, before flicking her eyes skyward and waving him towards a parking space instead. Then the two of them entered the estate through the little side-door and began the walk down the driveway. Pike was as usual dressed immaculately, in a short red leather skirt and matching jacket. Her high-heeled stiletto shoes didn't take too well to the potholes, though, and she vowed that the first thing she'd do when she took over Shipley Manor would be to build a proper road down to the house. Hadn't the fools heard of cars?

Tutt was dressed more practically and carried a small rucksack on his back, in which he kept his white inspection hat, his white inspection overalls and the white inspection gloves he would wear on his tour of the kitchens. He had a grey moustache the size and shape of a large postage stamp, grey wavy hair and glasses which were so thick that they made his eyes look like white billiard balls. Even with his glasses on, his eyesight was quite poor, but this only served to make him extra thorough. It was because of his poor eyesight that he looked at everything twice as closely, poking his long pointed nose into every suspicious nook and cranny twice as far as any normal inspector. Nothing, but nothing, got past him. Ever. In his left hand he carried one of the tools of his trade, his beloved clipboard. This he took with him wherever he went – even when he wasn't working. And he was already making notes in it, with a red biro specially selected for the day's work from his extensive private collection.

Gates locked – breach of emergency services access. Potholes in driveway – check 1971 Highways and Byways Act for possible breach of care and maintenance regulations.
Overhanging trees – check Council By-Law 36, relating to falling branches . . .

And so he went on, with the occasional shake of his head and a 'Tut-tut-tut, that will never do'. By the time they reached the drawbridge at the bottom of the driveway, Mr Tutt had filled three whole pages.

The Captain was running inside one of the treadmills.

'Ahoy there!' he called loudly when they arrived. 'Just having a little exercise. You must be Mr Tutt. Welcome to Shipley Manor.' He stepped out of the treadmill and offered a sweaty hand for Mr Tutt to shake.

'And you are – ?'

'Venetia Pike, Chief Executive of Shipley Town Council,' Pike said, moving closer and holding out a hand for him to kiss, which he had little option but to do.

'And you must be the Captain,' she observed.

'Last time I looked,' joked the Captain.

'I've heard so much about you,' she continued. 'Which is why I thought I would accompany my inspector here today. I think it's sssso important for the Chief Executive to meet the more, shall we say, *distinguished* members of our community.'

The Captain blushed slightly and, for once, was lost for words. He led his visitors over the drawbridge into the house, while Pike explained that the Council needed to undertake a routine inspection of Shipley Manor simply to ensure that it complied with all the necessary rules and regulations. Somehow it had been overlooked on previous occasions, but it was certainly nothing to worry about – 'just a formality,' as she put it. Mr Tutt, she said, would conduct the official inspection and, if the Captain had no objection, she would like an informal tour of the property, as it was clearly so beautiful.

'Perhaps this young lady would be kind enough to show me around,' she said, swivelling on the heel of a stiletto to look straight at Polly, who had been following at what she thought was a safe distance. Now she had little choice but to join them. If Pike was taken aback by Polly's appearance, she certainly wasn't showing it. Today, Polly was dressed from head to toe in bright orange, with her hair once again pulled up in thick strands at least two feet above her head, only this time in green.

'Polly's our resident fashion expert,' explained the Captain, then turning to her said, 'Nice carrot, Polly!'

She smiled at the compliment, at which point Mr Tutt cleared his throat, as if to say 'Remember me?', and Pike got down to business.

'Perhaps we'd better let Mr Tutt begin his inspection,' she suggested. 'Captain, if you would be good enough to show him around, I'm sure Polly will look after me very well indeed.'

And so they went their separate ways. Polly often showed people around Shipley Manor, but on this occasion she felt nervous. There was something peculiar about Venetia Pike. She walked with stiff, peacock-like steps, the result of strutting around on six-inch heels for years, but that wasn't it. Somehow she didn't seem quite . . . real. For example, her face looked quite young, the skin pulled over the bones, making it smooth and tight. But then her saggy neck reminded Polly of old Constance. Her hands did too. They were wrinkled, with thin and knobbly fingers – but in that case why did she have such glamorous young fingernails? Nothing seemed to fit. Most unsettling of all, though, was her smile. Fixed in position the whole time she was talking, it seemed stretched in some way, and even though it was a big smile with lots of teeth, her eyes didn't wrinkle up at the corners like the Captain's and her mother's did. Nevertheless, she had a job to do, so she answered Pike's endless questions as best she could. The Chief Executive seemed particularly interested in the fact that Polly didn't attend school. Polly explained that she was taught at Shipley Manor, by the Captain, Slugbucket, Seymour Boff and her mother. Her lessons included Drawing, Inventing, Making, Growing, Cooking, Recycling and Seafaring.

'No geography?' asked Pike. 'No history, no maths, no science?'

'No,' replied Polly, 'but the Captain says that any child who can plot a course across the Atlantic, taking account of wind speeds, ocean currents and the curvature of the earth, has a better education than most.'

'Does he indeed?' said Pike. 'Howww interesting . . .'

She then went on to ask Polly about the children who came to stay in the summer. Who looked after them? Were they supervised? Is it true they worked in the kitchens and gardens . . . for no pay? Polly tried to explain that it wasn't really work. It was more like fun than work: inventing and baking new kinds of cakes and biscuits, digging up vegetables to make giant pots of soup, that kind of thing. And once a week Slugbucket would hold a competition to see who could collect the most slugs to put in his bucket.

'It's a bit like an Easter-egg hunt, except that you're not allowed to eat them afterwards,' she said. 'But there are always prizes instead, like bottles of Fizzle to take home.'

Pike had been hoping that Polly would mention the water. Polly explained that it came up from the ground, where the Captain had dug the first hole for the moat, and that Seymour had eventually managed to control the flow and divert it through the existing water pipes. They used it for everything. It was brilliant for washing and cleaning, because the bubbles fizzed around so much that they loosened the dirt on clothes and practically licked it off the dishes. Bath time felt so nice that there was always a queue for the bathrooms, and Slugbucket could grow just about anything in the garden, so long as he could water it with Fizzle. The only problem came when you tried to cook with it. It lost some of its fizz when you boiled it, but not all, so soups and cups of tea retained a little sparkle, which took some getting used to. The best thing about it, though, was that it was magical. When asked to explain, Polly suggested that Pike try some for herself, so they came in from the garden and went down to the Captain's Cocktail Lounge. Polly poured a glass for the visitor and sat back to watch her drink it.

'Don't tell me, let me guess,' said Pike, closing her eyes and pressing her fingers into her temples in mock concentration. 'It gives you the power to read other people's minds.'

Polly looked at her hard, as if she was trying to do just that.

'Sometimes,' she replied.

A twitch of concern crossed Pike's face, but it was obvious that Polly couldn't see inside her head. How could she? The whole idea of magic water was utterly absurd.

'Well, it's certainly working, Polly,' she lied, 'because I can see you're thinking it's time for me to let you go and eat your lunch.'

And with that she thanked Polly for her help and said she would find her own way out. When she'd gone, Polly poured herself a glass of Fizzle and drank it slowly, watching the Fizzlefish through the portholes. If she *had* been able to read Pike's scheming mind, it would have sent shivers down her spine.

A Bad Report

'It's a disaster waiting to happen.'

Mr Tutt plopped his Shipley Manor inspection report on to Pike's desk. It was an inch thick and made Pike's teacup and saucer rattle when it landed. Ten days had passed since the inspection. Mr Tutt normally allowed himself at least three weeks to write his reports, but on this occasion Pike had been particularly keen for him to finish it.

'Thank you, Mr Tutt,' she said as he turned to leave. 'Very thorough.'

It was the greatest compliment anyone could pay him, and he left the room with the satisfied smile of a job well done. Pike picked up the report and flipped straight to the back, where Mr Tutt had written his conclusion.

For many years Shipley Manor has managed to evade all rules and regulations pertaining to the maintenance and running of local businesses. In the areas of Health & Safety, Food & Hygiene and Building Standards its facilities fall short of every statutory Council requirement and need to be upgraded. In view of the seriousness of the case I recommend that Shipley Manor be given one month – the minimum allowed – to carry out the urgent improvements listed in this report. Should a follow-up inspection at that time determine that they have failed to comply with its findings then, in the interests of Public Safety, I recommend that Shipley Manor be closed down.

Leonard Tutt
Chief Council Inspector, Shipley Town Council.

Got 'em! thought Pike gleefully.

Tom and Polly were sitting on the steps of Slugbucket's caravan. It was an old-fashioned gypsy caravan with a barrel-shaped roof, four wooden cartwheels and a stable-type door at the front, from which three wooden steps led down to the ground. The caravan had been the Captain's idea. After the Great Storm, Slugbucket had devoted all his time to restoring the woods. The caravan was intended to be a mobile shed that could be towed to whichever part of the woods Slugbucket was working on. In it he could store his heavy chainsaw and other woodcrafting tools, shelter from bad weather and take well-earned naps without having to go back to his room in the house. Slugbucket liked the caravan so much that, years later, his work on the Beastlybark Trail completed, he towed it to the bottom of the woods, close to the house and his tool shed, and made it his home.

Today, as both of them had finished their work, Polly was teaching Tom how to play Jumblupp. She was sitting on the top step of the caravan and Tom was on the bottom one, stroking Nautipus, who had come to watch. The step in between them was covered with small flat pebbles, each of which Polly had collected from the seashore and hand-painted with different letters of the alphabet.

'No, no, it's the complete opposite,' Polly was explaining. 'The whole idea is to make up words that *don't* exist. What's the point in coming up with words that someone has already thought of? This is much more fun.'

Tom found this a difficult idea to accept. After all, wasn't the whole point of word games to use real words, which you could check in a dictionary to see if they were right or wrong?

'How do you score, then?' he asked.

'Oh that's easy,' Polly explained. 'First of all you

get a point for each letter you use in your made-up word, so if you use all eight letters, you get eight points. Then you get marked out of eight for how good your word's definition is. If your word matches your definition exactly, then you get another eight points. Sixteen points is the maximum score. I've got that lots of times, like when I invented Nautipus's name. I used all my eight letters and said that Nautipus was a name for a mischievous ship's cat. The Captain gave me full marks for that one. Of course, if your opponent challenges you and finds your word in the dictionary, then you get no points at all. So are you ready for a game? The first to collect a hundred points is the winner.'

As Tom was new to Jumblupp, they decided that Polly should go first. She put the pebbles into a purple velvet bag, gave it a little shake, then drew eight of them out. She placed them carefully on the middle step. They were U-U-K-Y-Y-P-F-F.

'Oh, bad luck,' Tom commiserated. 'That's really difficult.'

'Not in Jumblupp,' said Polly. 'Don't forget you can make up anything you like, so long as you can explain what it means.' She shuffled the pebbles around for a few seconds, trying different combinations, then appeared to have a flash of inspiration.

'Got it,' she said, and rearranged the tiles to spell 'yukypuff'.

'What on earth's a "yukypuff"?' asked Tom.

'I'll give you a clue,' said Polly, before pinching her nose with her thumb and forefinger and screwing her face up in mock disgust, as if there was a bad smell in the air. 'Tom's done a yukypuff, Tom's done a yukypuff,' she sang, far too loudly for Tom's liking.

'All right, I get it, Polly,' he said quickly. 'That's quite a good word for it, actually. So how many extra points do you get for the definition?'

'Eight,' she said, 'because I think it fits the word perfectly. So, sixteen versus zero,' she went on, handing him the bag. 'Your turn.'

Tom dipped his hand into the bag and took out eight more pebbles, which he laid on the step. He stared at them in disbelief. He had pulled out eight letter Os.

'How in the Seven Seas did you do that?' Polly marvelled. 'I've never seen that happen before.'

Tom continued to stare at them, still unable to believe his eyes.

'It must be magic,' Polly stated confidently.

That was enough to break Tom out of his trance.

'You know I don't believe in magic,' he said rather seriously. 'It's obviously just a fluke. Statistically, once every thousand goes, or ten thousand goes, the pebbles are bound to come out all the same. I just happened to be the person taking that particular go, that's all.'

He looked up at Polly. Her lips were pushed tight together and she was almost purple from trying not to laugh. Then Tom realised.

'You switched bags!'

Polly exploded with laughter, rocking backwards and retrieving the original bag from its hiding place behind her. She dangled it from side to side in front of Tom's face, beside herself with pleasure.

'Very funny,' said Tom – and then, despite his best attempts not to, he started to laugh as well.

It wasn't something he did very often – somehow even laughing seemed wrong most of the time – but there was no denying how good it felt.

Unfortunately, their laughter was cut short by Seymour's voice booming out from the Crow's Nest.

'The second post has arrived, Polly.'

It was the message they'd been waiting for. Polly stood up and waved to Seymour to show that she'd heard him.

'Come on,' she said.

They walked up to collect the mail from the post-box. Almost two weeks had passed since Mr Tutt's inspection, and Polly had checked the mail every day hoping that the inspection results would be there. And today was the day. Sitting inside the post-box was a large brown envelope marked 'Official – From Shipley Town Council' and addressed to the Captain.

'We'd better take it to him straight away,' she said.

They found the Captain in the kitchen, chopping up onions to make soup. He was wearing diving goggles to stop his eyes from watering.

'Ooh, I wonder what this is,' he said jokingly, removing the goggles. He took the white tea-towel from over his shoulder, wiped his hands and put on his reading glasses. Polly handed him the envelope. At first he held it up to the light to examine it. Then he put it up to his ear and shook it.

'Well, it doesn't rattle, so there's no money in it,' he teased. Then he rested it in the palm of his hand as if to weigh it. 'I tell you what, though, it's pretty heavy – they must *really* like us.' Another joke.

Polly could tell that the Captain didn't want to open it. Why not? To her, Shipley Manor was the most wonderful place in the world, so how could anyone say anything bad about it? Eventually the Captain reached into his beard and pulled out a small pearl-handled penknife which he used to slit open the envelope. With a brief smile at Tom and Polly, he turned his attention to its contents.

Sir,

Improvement Order

Following a full and thorough inspection of your premises the Council has found Shipley Manor to be in serious breach of the 1948 Health and Safety at Work Act, the 1973 Food and Drink Act, the 1963 Building and Planning Regulations Act and Shipley Council By-Laws Numbers 5, 11, 13 and 24 (subsection 6). In order to comply with the above regulations substantial improvements are required in a number of areas. These are listed in the enclosed Schedule of Works. Because of the seriousness of these offences, all improvements must be completed within one month of today. If you fail to complete the work on time, Shipley Town Council will close Shipley Manor to the public forthwith. Our inspector will contact you in due course to arrange his follow-up inspection.

By order of Shipley Town Council

The Captain leaned back against the stone worktop and began reading the Council's Schedule of Works. Polly and Tom watched him carefully. First he raised his eyebrows in surprise. Then his mouth dropped open in astonishment. He frowned in bewilderment. He shook his head in disbelief. He gritted his teeth in anger.

'Shuddering shellfish!'

Finally he composed himself, and calmly placed the report back in its envelope.

'Polly, would you mind getting on the blowpipe and calling everyone down here?' he said. 'I think another meeting is called for.'

Five minutes later they were all seated at the kitchen table, and as soon as Maggie had finished pouring everyone a cup of tea, the Captain explained their position. They had one month to complete over a hundred improvements to Shipley Manor. Some of these were quite straightforward – like putting guard rails in front of the treadmills and fitting lights down the driveway. Others were more complicated: injecting the walls with foam insulation, for example, and fitting automatic water sprinklers in the cabins. Worst of all, the kitchen would need to be totally re-equipped, as none of the old ovens or fridges conformed to the latest Council standards. Even the beautiful stone worktop would need to be replaced by some new germ-resistant plastic. The problem with all this was twofold. First of all, they didn't have any money to buy the things they needed. Secondly, even if they did, they would need an army of helpers to get the work done in time.

'As I see it, we have two choices. Either we borrow enough money to buy all the help and equipment we need to finish the work on time, or we close Shipley Manor to the public and just keep the place to ourselves. No more families exploring the Beastlybark Trail. No more children staying in the cabins during the summer. Just us. I know money would be tight without any income from the cabins, but I'm sure we'd muddle along somehow.'

'Perhaps we could get a stall and sell things in Shipley market once a week,' suggested Maggie.

'Loik fruit 'n' veg fer starters,' Slugbucket offered. 'If oi stepped up production in me vegetable garden, oi reckon we'd 'ave loads left over.'

'And I could donate some of my special home-made jam,' added Constance.

'We could even sell some of my inventions,' suggested Seymour enthusiastically. 'I'm sure those refrigerated underpants I invented would sell like hot cakes in the summer.'

No one seemed entirely convinced about that.

'Well, I like people coming here,' declared Polly. 'It's such a wonderful place I want everyone to see it.'

Seymour turned to the Captain.

'The house belongs to you, Captain,' he said. 'What do you want to do?'

The Captain had already made up his mind.

'I agree with Polly,' he replied. 'I know it's not a ship, but everything else about Shipley Manor is so special that I think we should share it. I'll do whatever it takes to keep it open to the public. But make no mistake,' he continued, waving the Schedule of Works in the air, 'if we spend a fortune doing all this work it won't be easy to meet the monthly repayments. We'll need to triple the number of paying visitors during the summer and keep the cabins rented out all year round, apart from when we have the children staying. And of course, all this is assuming that someone will lend us the money in the first place.'

Tom, who had been feeling slightly apart from the proceedings as he was the only person who didn't live at Shipley Manor, suddenly found himself able to make a contribution.

'My father works in a bank, if that helps,' he said. 'Perhaps I could mention it to him.'

'Thank you, shipmate. That would be very helpful indeed,' replied the Captain. 'In the meantime, Seymour and I will take a closer look at this wretched document and work out exactly how many gold doubloons we're going to need.'

Grub's Killer Clause

On Monday morning Grub sat at his desk, gently tapping it with the end of his fountain pen and waiting for Tom's father to knock on the door. He knew that he would. He knew that Venetia Pike had sent the Schedule of Works to Shipley Manor. He knew that Roger's son worked there every weekend and that, if he was anything like his idiot father, he would try to help. In a few moments, Roger would be in his office asking him whether the bank could lend Shipley Manor the money they so desperately needed. He knew all this. He was like a master puppeteer, and Tom and Roger were his poor, dumb puppets, dancing to his tune and, though they didn't know it, helping to make him filthy, stinking, gloriously rich. There was a knock on the door.

'Come in, Roger,' he shouted.

The meeting was brief. Roger was in and out of Grub's office in less than three minutes, a little puzzled at how helpful Grub had been, but nevertheless pleased with the result. Meanwhile, Grub phoned Venetia Pike to give his 'darling fluffy bunny' the good news – the trap was closing around Shipley Manor. He would pay them a visit tomorrow and arrange to lend them the money.

The following morning Grub parked his gleaming gold sports car at the top of the driveway and began the walk down to Shipley Manor. It was quite a warm day, and by the time he crossed the drawbridge to the main door little beads of sweat were racing each other down the sides of his face. He paused to regain his breath and looked up at the magnificent building in front of him. Suddenly, all thought of turning it into a luxury hotel vanished, and was replaced by a far greater vision. Imagine. Imagine if Shipley Manor became his home, so that *he* was 'Lord of the Manor' instead of that idiot Captain Shipley. Imagine the respect. Imagine people no longer laughing at him for being short and fat and balding. Imagine, even, his darling Venetia agreeing to marry him and become Lady Grub. Just *imagine* it. The thought invigorated him, and he felt a sudden over-whelming urge to do business. He treated himself to a generous splash of 'Eau d'Executive' and stepped up to the door. Grasping the dolphin-shaped door knocker by the tail, he gave it three loud knocks. A few moments later he heard footsteps on the other side, then Polly's face appeared in the hatch. Grub introduced himself and told her that he knew the Captain was interested in taking out a bank loan. Normally, he said, he would wait to make an appointment, but he just happened to be passing on his way to see another customer (the first of his many lies that day) and thought he would stop off at Shipley Manor to offer his services. He reached into his black executive briefcase and pulled out a business card which he handed to Polly. She looked at it carefully, then let him in and asked him to wait in the corridor while she went to fetch the Captain. As usual, she found him in the kitchen preparing a meal. 'There's a bank manager called Barclay Grub to see you, Captain,' she said, handing him the card. 'He smells funny.'

The Captain hurried out into the corridor to meet him.

'Good morning, Mr Grub,' he said, offering the bank manager a bright orange hand to shake.

Grub hesitated and the Captain realised that his

hand was still covered in curry spice.

'Oh, I do beg your pardon,' he apologised, taking the tea-towel from his shoulder and wiping his hands. 'I was in the middle of making a curry for lunch. Now let's find somewhere to sit down.'

The Captain led the way to his cabin and skipped over the wobbly barrels on to the raft. He sat down in his chair and urged Grub to follow him.

'The knack is to jump from one to the other quickly,' he advised, 'before they have time to wobble.'

But Grub wasn't very good at taking advice. He found himself standing on the first barrel with his arms outstretched, trying desperately to keep his balance and remain still. Each time the barrel moved in one direction, he lurched in the other to counterbalance it and stop himself from falling. But that only made the barrel wobble even more. And whenever he managed to stop it wobbling from side to side, it immediately started wobbling backwards and forwards instead. Within a few seconds his arms were spinning round like the sails of a windmill in a Force Nine gale. And then, just when he thought things couldn't get any worse, they did. His briefcase burst wide open, sending his papers flying into the air like white doves out of a magician's hat. Worst of all, the wisps of hair which normally stretched over the top of his bald head had fallen in front of his eyes like a greasy black curtain. So he was completely stuck: unable to get off, unable to stand still, unable to jump to the next barrel – and now unable to see. If it hadn't been covered by fallen hair, Grub's crimson face would have told the Captain exactly how he felt about this whole embarrassing experience. How dare that jumped-up ferryboat captain with his stupid chef's hat and his ridiculous uniform make a laughing stock out of me, he was fuming. How dare he? I'll make him pay. He'll regret the day he ever set eyes on Barclay Grub!

But the Captain wasn't laughing at all.

'My dear chap, I'm so sorry,' he said, as he helped Grub down from the barrel. 'I'm so used to them that sometimes I forget just how difficult they are to balance on. Here, let me pick this lot up for you.'

The Captain bent down and retrieved Grub's paperwork from the floor, unaware that it had been written specially for him by his visitor. As he shuffled it back into a neat pile, he couldn't help noticing how small the type was.

'You must have pretty good eyesight to read this lot, Mr Grub,' he said jovially. 'Have you ever thought of becoming a ship's lookout?'

Grub managed a weak smile, and started stuffing

the papers back into his empty briefcase.

A minute later the Captain and Mr Grub were sitting at opposite sides of the desk. The Captain wedged a copy of *Celestial Navigation for Seafarers* under the corner of the raft to stop it from wobbling, then poured Grub a tall glass of Fizzle.

So *this* is the famous magic water, thought Grub, taking a sip. Well, it doesn't taste very magical to me.

But he found it quite reviving, and he soon recovered his composure enough to begin the meeting. The Captain told Grub about Mr Tutt's inspection and showed him the list of improvements which needed to be carried out if Shipley Manor was to be allowed to stay open. He also explained that he needed the money straightaway because they had been given just one month to complete the work. Finally, he told him how he intended to repay the loan.

'We're going to advertise,' he said. 'We're going to tell everyone how wonderful Shipley Manor is and triple the number of visitors coming through the gates during the summer. That should generate enough extra money every month to repay the loan.'

Grub listened to all this with his lips pursed tightly together and his head shaking from side to side in mock sympathy.

'How could the Council treat you like that?' he kept repeating. 'It's disgraceful, absolutely disgraceful.'

When the Captain had finished, Grub took another sip of Fizzle before reaching into his briefcase.

'I'm sure the bank can help you, Captain Shipley. Purely by chance,' he lied again, 'I have a spare loan contract here in my briefcase.'

An hour later the Captain returned to his kitchen a happy man. Tucked into the rim of his chef's hat was a cheque from the bank. He took it out and gave it a little kiss. If he was careful, it would cover the cost of all the improvements and still leave a little left over for emergencies. He folded it in half and popped it into his apron pocket alongside the loan contract which Grub had given him to sign.

The contract contained eight pages of densely packed type which explained the bank's rules and regulations about lending money. Buried deep within them, concealed among the thousands of tiny, almost invisible words, was one extra condition which Grub had inserted especially for his victim. He thought of this as his Killer Clause. The Captain had signed the contract that afternoon. He hadn't read it properly because the type was so small, but he had been happy to trust Barclay Grub's crooked assurances that everything in it was completely normal, and that he would be able to repay the loan in easy monthly instalments. Perhaps one day he would find his magnifying glass and look at it more closely. Not now, though. He had a curry to finish making. Polly's favourite.

Closed for Repairs

Polly was teaching Tom how to use the mechanical digger. At first he couldn't believe she was allowed to operate it by herself, but nothing about Shipley Manor surprised him that much any more, and Slugbucket had assured him that Polly was an experienced and responsible driver. So there he was at the controls, being taught how to dig a drainage ditch by a girl dressed up as a sunflower. One week remained before Mr Tutt's second inspection and, however much he tried to pretend otherwise, Tom was having the time of his life. The Captain had decided to close Shipley Manor for the whole month so that they could concentrate on completing all the improvements in time. He had offered Tom as much extra work as he could manage, so every weekend and for an hour or two after school most days, he caught the bus to Shipley Manor. He never knew what new task he would be given. He had climbed trees to lop off dangerous branches, he had shinned up drainpipes to touch up rusty paintwork and he had sat astride the pitched roofs of the cabins hammering in nails to secure roof felting which had come loose in the wind. In the cabins, it had been his job to make sure that every tap, every light, every heater and every electric socket was in perfect working order, so he'd worked closely with plumbers and electricians and an army of other skilled workers that the Captain had hired, to make sure that their work was carried out properly. Tom enjoyed making everything neat and tidy to meet the Council's Rules and Regulations. But, secretly, what put the biggest smile on his face was being free – in fact, *required* – to do things like climb trees and clamber over rooftops in order to do so.

Every evening, Tom returned home exhausted and happy, and sat down at the kitchen table with his father to eat a hot supper and share the day's events. Well, most of them. In turn, the next day Barclay Grub, feigning interest in Tom's welfare, would gently prod and probe the unwitting Roger for snippets of information about progress at Shipley Manor. And as the weeks passed, he didn't like what he was hearing. The work seemed to be going too well, and all on budget. He didn't want Shipley Manor to pass the inspection. He wanted them to fall at the first hurdle, to fail it miserably and be closed down by Mr Tutt for good.

Without any hope of earning money from visitors, it would then be impossible for the Captain to repay even part of the bank loan, let alone the whole amount, which Grub was preparing to demand from him. He couldn't wait to see the Captain's ashen face when he realised that the date on the contract – exactly two weeks after Mr Tutt's second inspection – wasn't the date of the first monthly repayment, as Grub had told him, but the day the loan, plus astronomical interest, had to be paid back *in full*. What a glorious moment that would be! Surpassed only when he pointed out to the Captain that if he couldn't pay up, Clause 8, Paragraph 9, Subsection 3 of the loan contract, which he'd signed willingly just a few weeks before, clearly stated that every brick, blade of grass and bunny rabbit at Shipley Manor would belong to the bank.

He would then give him one hour to come up with the money, during which time the Captain would receive a mysterious phone call from the

Shipley Property Investment Company, offering to rescue him. The muffled voice on the phone would offer a rock-bottom price for Shipley Manor, but it *would* be enough for the Captain to repay the bank and take his family off to live in a tiny cottage somewhere. It would be better than ending up with nothing, so Grub was confident that the Captain, like every victim before him, would have to accept it. Then he and his darling Venetia could become Lord and Lady of the Manor. The perfect ending.

First things first, though, he reminded himself. He and Venetia wouldn't take any chances. Any attempt to relaunch Shipley Manor Country Club and turn it into a successful business had to be thwarted. Unfortunately, with a week to go the Captain seemed well on course to pass the inspection with flying colours. So Grub picked up the phone and called Pike. What they needed was a way to make sure that Shipley Manor would fail the inspection, no matter what. Something foolproof.

'Don't worry, Barclay,' she assured him. 'I'm way ahead of you.'

Venetia Pike had been shopping. Normally she wouldn't be seen dead in a smelly old second-hand clothes shop, but this was different. This was business. She kicked the front door shut behind her and carried the two large bags straight upstairs to her attic. Once there she switched on the light and walked across the smooth white tiled floor to put the bags down by a gleaming white dressing table. Above the dressing table was a large oval mirror, surrounded by twenty light bulbs which illuminated Pike's face from every angle. She stood back and admired the view. But on this occasion she wasn't looking at herself. On either side of the dressing table, and above it, were row upon row of old computer screens, arranged on metal shelves which stretched all the way to the ceiling. Dozens of them. Each one had bleeped 'Do You Want To Quit?' once too often for Pike's liking and had suffered the final indignity of having its plug pulled out for good.

'Hello, boys,' she said to them. 'Mummy's home.'

The air prickled with expectancy. She stepped forward and placed the palm of her hands against each screen in turn, occasionally pressing her painted lips to the glass. But these were no longer computer monitors as we know them. Their insides had been wrenched out and discarded and their tops sliced open and transformed into lids. Where once they were filled with circuit boards and hard disks, they now contained little lights and heaters.

Today they had new lives . . . as terrariums, home to Venetia Pike's only real friends, her collection of hissing, writhing and mostly poisonous snakes.

The snakes were waking up now, coming out from their hiding places behind rocks and plastic plants to press their noses against the glass and flick their tongues in greeting. They could smell her. They could see her. And even though snakes are deaf, they could feel the familiar vibration of her voice. She dipped her hand into one of the terrariums, pulling it out moments later with a baby grass snake coiled tight around her bony wrist, like a shimmering green bracelet. Living jewellery, she thought admiringly. The height of ssssophistication.

'Have you been esssspecially good today?' she asked it. 'Have you earned your ssssupper?'

She dropped the snake back into its home, then moved over to a bench at the side of the room and removed three tubs from the small freezer underneath it. The first contained rigid white mice, their front feet curled up as if they were enjoying a warm, carefree sleep. The second tub, much larger, contained six brown rats, and inside the third was a single small sparrow. This was a special treat, a tasty little morsel for Venetia Pike's best friend, her boa constrictor Viceroy. Pike tipped the morbid contents on to a plastic tray to thaw out, then from a cupboard on the opposite side of the room she took out a round cake tin. Its lid was punched through with dozens of tiny air holes. She prised it open and inspected the contents. Worms. Hundreds and hundreds of them, moving in and out and around each other like live spaghetti.

You can't beat a bit of fresh produce, she thought to herself as she replaced the lid and put the tin on the bench with the rest of the food.

'Not long now, boys,' she said, looking up at the shelves. 'Be patient.'

She pulled a white swivel stool from underneath the dressing table and sat down facing the mirror. She was ready to dismantle herself. First, she gripped the top of her head and pulled. Her white-blonde hair lifted off in her hands. She placed the wig on a stand to the side of the dressing table and rubbed her scalp with the tips of her fingers. Her real hair was short, grey and patchy, like the little clumps of grass that poke through sand dunes at the beach. Next she removed her long red fingernails and placed them carefully in a glass dish in front of her. These were soon joined by a pair of long black eyelashes which she peeled from her eyelids with surgical precision. Then she went to the corner of the room and washed her face in the sink, removing all traces of make-up before patting her face dry with a towel and returning to her seat.

She was now unrecognisable to anyone other than her snakes. Only they were ever allowed to see her like this. Because only they were her equals – expert, like her, at slipping silently up to their prey and striking without warning or mercy. And it was only they, she had decided, who could give Mr Tutt such an unforgettable fright during his inspection tomorrow morning that he would order Shipley Manor to stay closed for good, no matter what they had done to improve the place. Venetia Pike reached down for the first carrier bag. It was time to transform herself.

The Captain sat alone at his desk studying Mr Tutt's Schedule of Works one last time before tomorrow's inspection. Everyone at Shipley Manor had worked their socks off over the past month, and he and Seymour had double-checked every single item of work on the list. Everything had been completed. Everything was shipshape. Confident that there was nothing more that could be done, he closed the Schedule of Works and was about to sit back in his chair and relax when he heard a knock on the main door.

Leaping lobsterpots, he thought, looking at his pocket watch. Who can that be at this time of night?

He made his way down the corridor and opened

the door. A woman he'd never seen before was standing on the drawbridge, peering at him from behind a pair of black-rimmed glasses. Her face was framed by a floral headscarf tied firmly beneath her chin, and on her feet a pair of open-toed leather sandals exposed a set of knobbly white toes. Over the shoulder of her drab brown overcoat, a large zip-up tapestry bag strained to contain its bulging contents.

'I do apologise for calling on you so late,' the woman said. 'My name is Matilda Goode. I'm director of an organisation called Holidays for City Kids and I've heard such good reports about Shipley Manor from a very dear friend of mine. Perhaps you know him – his name is Barclay Grub.'

'Oh, indeed I do,' replied the Captain.

'Well, that's why I'm calling,' she continued. 'I'm touring the area looking for places to send our children later this year. Mr Grub recommended you so highly that I thought I must pay you a visit before returning to the city. I hope you don't mind.'

Naturally, the Captain couldn't possibly turn away such a sweet, kind lady, no matter what time it was.

'Not in the least, you're very welcome,' he responded enthusiastically. 'Come aboard.'

The Captain led Matilda Goode inside. 'Now, what would you like to see first?' he said.

'I'm particularly keen to see the kitchens,' she answered quickly. 'Food is such an important aspect of growing children's lives, don't you agree, Captain?'

'I most certainly do,' he replied. 'And I think our kitchen will impress you – it's recently undergone a complete refurbishment. We're going to get down to some pretty serious cooking in there this year if I have anything to do with it.'

He hurried Matilda Goode into the kitchen, holding the door open for her with one hand and stretching his other arm out with a flourish. 'Our new kitchen,' he announced proudly.

Matilda Goode began to look around. Although she seemed oddly engrossed with opening drawers and looking inside containers, the Captain didn't mind at all. He felt sure she would be impressed, because he knew that everything in there shone like a new pin. But Matilda Goode wasn't looking for grease and grime. She was searching for places in which to empty the contents of her bag. Somewhere safe. Somewhere escape-proof. Somewhere that would remain undisturbed until Mr Tutt stuck his official nose in first thing in the morning. That should wake him up a bit, she thought gleefully – like a cold shower with fangs.

All she had to do now was get rid of the Captain. And soon too, because she could feel her bag getting restless.

'Captain,' she said at last, 'I'll be fine by myself if you want to answer it.'

The Captain looked puzzled.

'The door,' she explained. 'I'm sure I just heard someone knock.'

'Did you?' replied the Captain. 'You know, I must get my ears tested one of these days. I didn't hear a thing. I'll be right back – please make yourself at home.'

He left the room and in a flash Matilda Goode reached up and took down the flour tin. She removed the lid. Good – it was empty. She took the tapestry bag from her shoulder and in one fluid movement unzipped the top and tipped its contents straight into the tin, replacing the lid just as she heard the Captain's footsteps returning. She still had a few more seconds. She opened the drawer in front of her and searched around frantically. At last she found what she was looking for. A skewer. She raised it above her head, then, with all the force she could manage, she hammered the sharp point down on to the lid, making a puncture hole just large enough to let in some air.

'I want you to be alive and kicking when Mr Tutt finds you,' she whispered to the tin as she placed it back on the shelf. A split second later, Polly appeared in the doorway. She was on her way to bed and had stopped off to say goodnight to the Captain. Matilda Goode froze mid-step as their eyes met, and Polly was suddenly overcome by a deep woozy feeling in the pit of her stomach, just as she had been when she met Venetia Pike a month before. Something didn't feel right but, then again, perhaps she was merely suffering from pre-inspection nerves. Then the Captain reappeared.

'Oh Polly, I see you've met Matilda Goode. With a bit of luck Matilda will be our first new customer when we reopen.'

Matilda Goode smiled at Polly, who smiled back hesitantly before wishing them both goodnight and disappearing to bed. The visitor turned back to the Captain.

'Well, there was no one there,' he informed her with a friendly shrug of his shoulders. 'Perhaps you heard a woodpecker working late. We have quite a few of those in the woods, you know. Now, let's get on with this guided tour, shall we?'

An hour later Matilda Goode returned to her attic to remove her disguise. She unbuckled her shoes and held them at arm's length between her thumb and forefinger.

'Talk about a bad attack of open-toed sandals,' she sneered, before dropping them into Viceroy's terrarium. 'Chew on those, ssssweetie.' She moved over the cold tiles to her dressing table and sat down. She removed her headscarf, tilting her head from side to side to inspect each individual clump of grey hair in the mirror. Then she lifted the white-blonde wig from its stand next to her, and fitted it carefully and expertly back on her head. Finally, she picked up a stick of bright crimson lipstick and applied a thick coating to her top lip.

'Goodbye, Matilda Goode,' she said, pursing her lips together to spread the colour. 'Welcome back, Venetia Pike.'

Polly lay in her bed staring up at the ceiling. It was midnight. She felt uneasy, unable to sleep. The thought of Mr Tutt's visit in the morning was keeping her awake. Everyone else seemed confident that Shipley Manor would pass the inspection, but her queasy tummy wasn't so sure. What if Mr Tutt found something which hadn't been done properly? Or worse still, what if he discovered that something hadn't been done at all? What if Shipley Manor had to stay shut – how would they repay the money to the bank if they weren't allowed to open for visitors? And why did the woman in the kitchen trouble her so much? Why did she seem so familiar . . . was it something about the way she moved? Endless questions raced around inside her head.

Perhaps if she got up and had something to eat she would be able to sleep afterwards. She smiled to herself . . . how very sensible, Tom *would* approve.

Quietly, so that she wouldn't wake Calypso in the nursery next door, she slipped out of her bedroom. Lighting her way with a small wind-up torch, she padded barefoot down to the kitchen on the floor below. She opened the door, pleased to hear that its newly oiled hinges no longer squeaked, and stood in the doorway, shining her torch from side to side like a searchlight looking for escaped prisoners. Perhaps something from the fridge. Or the larder maybe. Then her torch beam settled on the wooden bread bin, and she decided to make herself a sandwich. She tiptoed over the bare floorboards and pushed the lid open. It was empty. Never mind, a biscuit would do. She shone her torch along the shelf above the bread bin, hoping the biscuit tin would be in its usual place. Sure enough, the familiar blue flour tin – which hadn't been used to store flour for many years – was sitting there, in between the coffee jar and the tea caddy. She would need two hands, so she put the torch down and reached up to the high shelf. She held the tin with her right hand and pulled the lid off with a loud 'plop'. Slowly she lowered her other hand inside to feel around for a biscuit. Funny, she thought. At that moment she felt a sharp pain in her little finger, as if it had been stabbed with a white-hot needle. Instinctively, she pulled her hand away, catching the top of the tin and tipping it with a loud clatter on to its side. Six hissing snakes spilled out on to her, knocking her backwards on to the hard floor. Polly screamed.

Oh, how she screamed.

Within seconds the Captain was in the doorway. He turned on the light just in time to see the last snake fall from Polly's body and slither away underneath a cupboard. He rushed over to her and scooped her frightened, shivering body up in his arms. A few moments later, Polly felt a second pair of arms around her.

'What on earth's happened?' asked Maggie.

'There was a snake in here,' replied the Captain. 'It must have come in from the garden. I saw it go underneath that cupboard.' He nodded towards the corner of the room. At last Polly spoke.

'There were lots of them,' she shivered, holding up her red and swollen finger, 'and one of them bit me – look.'

Maggie took Polly from the Captain and held

her tightly. She was as white as a sheet.

'Don't worry, Polly, you're going to be fine', she whispered. 'I've got some special medicine upstairs left over from when Slugbucket was building the Beastlybark Trail. He was bitten lots of times rummaging around underneath all those old tree-trunks. Now let's get you sorted out, shall we?'

Before leaving she turned back to the Captain.

'I'll look after Polly,' she said to him quietly. 'You take care of the snakes.'

He smiled at her.

'I get all the best jobs,' he said as he closed the door securely behind them, so that none of the snakes could escape. It was going to be a long night. If they didn't get rid of every single one of those snakes before Mr Tutt's inspection first thing tomorrow morning – well, that would be it, wouldn't it? They'd be sunk. No more Shipley Manor Country Club. No more 'Cabins for Kids'. He reached for the kitchen blowpipe.

'All hands on deck,' he bellowed.

Hide and Seek

Venetia Pike had thought long and hard about what to leave in the kitchen for Mr Tutt to find. Much as she was tempted to surprise him with something wildly exotic and highly deadly, like a king cobra or a diamondback rattlesnake, she had decided against it. After all, he wouldn't be much use to her lying dead, face down on the kitchen floor. She needed him scared witless, but well enough afterwards to write the most damning Council inspection report in the history of damning Council inspection reports. She needed something that would give him a nasty nip, but leave him standing long enough to order Shipley Manor to close its snake-infested doors to the public for ever. And there was one other consideration. The only cobras and rattlesnakes to be found in England were in zoos and private collections like hers. If one suddenly turned up at Shipley Manor then suspicions would be aroused. Sabotage might be suspected. And she certainly didn't want that. No, she'd have to go for something local, something that could simply have wandered into the kitchen from the nearby woods. Grass snakes. There were plenty of them around in this part of England, and although they could give you a nasty bite, they weren't poisonous. Yes, a nice big handful of those would do the trick.

Maggie, though, didn't know what kind of snake had bitten Polly. The kitchen had been too dark for Polly to see it clearly, and the Captain had caught only the briefest glimpse. So she couldn't afford to take any chances. After leaving the kitchen she took Polly straight upstairs to her bedroom and laid her down on her bed. She wrapped a warm patchwork blanket around her and fetched a large first-aid box from the bathroom cabinet. She knew the snake was almost certain to have been a harmless grass snake, because they were by far the most common species in the area. But she decided to treat Polly for a poisonous adder bite, just in case. She cleaned and dressed Polly's wound, then injected a small dose of anti-venom into the base of her little finger. Polly didn't flinch, but as soon as it was over she held out her arms for her mum to join her, so Maggie climbed on to the bed, put her arms round her daughter and cuddled her until she fell into a dreamy sleep.

Polly was in her pyjamas, sitting cross-legged in the middle of the kitchen floor, facing the door. In front of her was a brown wicker basket. She heard footsteps approaching. For some reason she wanted to run away and hide, but she couldn't move. She watched as the kitchen door swung open and Matilda Goode stepped inside. She looked around her, then walked over and sat down opposite Polly, though she appeared not to see her. Then there were more footsteps. These were louder, more clicky, and they belonged to Venetia Pike. She strode into the room in her stiletto-heeled shoes which, like the tight green jumpsuit she wore, appeared to be made from snakeskin. She tilted her head back and quietly sniffed the air before joining Matilda Goode on the floor opposite Polly. She too appeared not to see her. Once again, Polly tried to stand up and run away, but her arms and legs wouldn't move. She looked down and saw the bandage on her little finger. Blood was starting to seep through it. Where was her mother?

Very slowly, Matilda Goode and Venetia Pike

turned their heads towards each other. When their eyes met they seemed to ignite, flaring into four of the brightest, most piercing green eyes that Polly had ever seen. And then they turned back to face Polly. But this time they could see her. Together, they stared deep into her eyes. 'Good evening, sssssssweeetie,' they hissed in unison. Then they floated upwards, an inch or two above the floor, before moving sideways into each other, merging together like two transparent ghosts occupying the same space. And then they became one – half Matilda Goode and half Venetia Pike. The woman that floated back down to earth opposite Polly still wore Venetia Pike's green snakeskin jumpsuit, but on her feet were Matilda Goode's brown leather open-toed sandals and on her head she wore the same flowery headscarf that Polly had seen earlier that evening. Only this time the headscarf was moving. The woman continued to look Polly in the eye, holding her gaze while she untied the knot under her chin and lifted off the scarf. Underneath, a dozen glistening black snakes squirmed and writhed around on her head like a living wig, hissing and spitting and baring their fangs at Polly. Then she reached into her tapestry bag and took out a silver flute. With her eyes still locked on Polly, she put the instrument to her lips and began to play. A few moments later the head of a large, deadly cobra appeared above the rim of the basket. It rose, swaying rhythmically, until it was the same height as Polly. Then it swivelled round to face her. Polly tried to raise her arms to shield herself, but she was paralysed, held tight inside an invisible straitjacket. She called for help, but the air around her seemed to catch her cries and dissolve them. There was nothing she could do. The cobra leaned forward until she could feel its cold, foul breath on the end of her nose, 'Ssssssay goodbye to Sssssssshipley Manor, sssssssssweetie,' it hissed. Then suddenly, without warning, it reared backwards and bared its long, razor-sharp fangs before launching itself at Polly.

Polly screamed – and woke up.

Maggie rushed in from the nursery where she had been feeding Calypso, but Polly was already sitting up, rubbing her eyes and yawning. Clearly she was much better.

'What time is it?' she asked.

'Six o'clock in the morning,' replied Maggie, perching on the edge of the bed and offering Polly a glass of Fizzle.

'Have they caught the snakes yet?'

'Only two so far,' replied her mother grimly. 'But at least they were only grass snakes, so it looks as though we've got you around for a little while longer.' She took Polly's hand and checked the bandage.

Polly made a quick calculation. That worked out at one snake every three hours. At that rate they'd never catch them all before Mr Tutt arrived.

'I've got to go down there,' Polly said urgently. 'My dream's just given me an idea.'

Maggie took Polly's temperature before giving her the all-clear. 'Off you go then,' she said. 'But put some boots on before you go into the kitchen.'

Polly jumped out of bed and went straight to her chest of drawers. Socks and pants flew everywhere as she scrabbled around in her top drawer, like a dog digging a hole. Then she found what she was looking for. It was the penny whistle that Slugbucket had given her for her birthday. Stopping only to grab her Fizzlestick and wellington boots from the wardrobe, she raced off to the kitchen.

The Captain answered the kitchen door when she knocked on it. He was wearing his white bee-keeping suit, with the hood up and the protective bee-keeping veil hanging down in front of his face. White elasticated gloves and boots were sealed tight around his wrists and ankles. Polly burst out laughing as soon as she saw him. He looked like a snowman.

'You may laugh, but I don't want anything long and slithery slipping down my neck now, do I?' the Captain explained from behind the veil, before lifting it up to greet Polly properly. 'Well, I'll be a bosun's mate, you look as good as new.'

'I've come to help,' said Polly, holding up her Fizzlestick and penny whistle.

'I won't pretend we don't need it,' he admitted. 'We've found another one of our unwelcome visitors hiding behind the fridge, but we can't persuade it to come out. The poor thing's frightened to death, I expect. Speaking of which,' he said, bending down to put a gloved hand on her shoulder, 'are you sure you're ready to face them? You had a nasty shock last night.'

Polly nodded and stepped past him into the kitchen. She saw Slugbucket lying on his back with one arm wedged behind the fridge. He looked up and waved a pink rubber-gloved hand at Polly before resuming his attempt to poke the snake out with a wooden spoon. Seymour sat in wait on the other side of the fridge, holding an upturned plastic dustbin, ready to drop it down over the snake as soon as Slugbucket chased it out into the open. He was frozen with concentration and didn't look up.

'This one just won't budge,' the Captain explained to Polly. 'We've been trying for half an hour now.'

'What you need is a snake charmer,' she announced confidently, blowing a couple of notes to show she was ready for action.

'Nice . . . thought, Polly,' grunted Slugbucket from the floor, 'but snakes is deaf. It's the rhythm of the . . . instrument, the way it . . . sways when you play it, that attracts 'em. This little fella would 'ave to see you, and 'e can't from . . . underneath . . . this bloomin' great . . . fridge.'

Polly looked dejected. Her great idea was in ruins.

'Fizzlesticks,' she muttered.

A second later, as if someone had flipped a switch, Seymour suddenly burst into life. 'Periscope!' he shouted, causing Slugbucket to bang his elbow on the corner of the fridge. 'We'll make a periscope. We'll use mirrors to send Polly's reflection underneath the fridge so the snake can see her.'

He dropped the dustbin on to the floor and whirled out of the room, returning shortly with two long mirrors balanced between the armrests on his wheelchair. They were the side mirrors from Edna's dressing table.

'I don't think she'll miss them,' he said. 'For some reason she doesn't spend much time doing her hair these days.'

'Now,' he continued enthusiastically, 'this is what we'll do . . .'

After a few instructions from Seymour, Slugbucket lifted Polly on to the fridge, where she was to sit and play the penny whistle. Then, under Seymour's direction, he held the first mirror in front of her and bounced her reflection down to the second mirror, which Seymour had propped up on the floor at precisely the right angle to send Polly's reflection underneath the fridge. Once Polly had charmed the snake into the open, the Captain was to scoop it up with the hook on Polly's Fizzlestick and drop it into the bin. Then Seymour would put the lid on. Simple. All Polly had to do now was play the penny whistle and remember to sway to the music. She put her fingers to the instrument and began to play a slow, rhythmic tune, moving from side to side as gracefully and hypnotically as she could. She knew that periscopes worked in reverse, and that if the snake could see her, she should also be able to see the snake, so she looked into the mirror in front of her for any signs of life. At first she could see nothing but darkness. But then she began to make out a shape, the coil of a snake perhaps. And then it saw her, and its bright green eyes, illuminated by reflected light, shone in her direction. Polly's heart started to beat faster as the snake moved slowly towards her. But she continued to play. She tried to remember that she was only looking at a reflection, and that the snake was still underneath the fridge, but in the mirror it seemed barely a foot away from her face. Still she played on. Suddenly, just like the deadly cobra in her dream, the snake looked her straight in the eye and lunged at her. She gasped and jerked backwards, but the snake was gone.

'Got you, my little beauty,' she heard the Captain say, followed by the comforting thud of Seymour slamming down the dustbin lid.

'Well done, Polly,' said the Captain. 'It worked like a dream.'

It certainly did, thought Polly, remembering the cobra. Her heart was still pounding as she jumped down from the fridge, but she liked the feeling. This was exciting. Much more fun than catching Fizzlefish.

The Captain checked his pocket watch.

They had one hour to go before Mr Tutt arrived, and so far they had caught just three snakes. Polly knew there were more. She'd felt them. But how many. One? Two? Surely there couldn't be more than that. And if there were, then where in the Seven Seas were they hiding? They had searched under every cooker, every fridge, every cupboard, they had checked every saucepan, emptied out every drawer, looked inside every storage jar and cereal box. They had searched everywhere.

'The only thing we haven't done is rip up the floorboards,' the Captain concluded.

They all looked at each other. No one liked the sound of that.

'I noticed a few holes behind the cupboard where they could have got under the boards,' he continued ominously.

'It makes sense, doesn't it?' said Seymour. 'I mean, any snake faced with us three waving wooden spoons and upside-down dustbins in the air is bound to head straight for the nearest dark hole.'

'Surely they must be getting hungry by now,' offered Polly. 'Perhaps we could lure them out with some bait?'

'Trouble is, we don't 'ave any,' said Slugbucket. 'All we got is 'alf a million slugs and they don't eat 'em. They likes mice 'n frogs 'n insects. But not slugs.'

'And we don't have time to take up the floorboards,' said the Captain, looking again at his pocket watch. 'The tide's coming in fast, shipmates.'

'What about Nautipus?' Polly asked Slugbucket. 'He likes catching things, doesn't he?'

'Don't talk to me about that bloomin' cat,' complained Slugbucket, shaking his head. 'I brought 'im in 'ere 'opin' 'e might catch 'em all in ten minutes and do you know what 'e done? Took one sniff, then turned 'imself around an' ran straight back out again. An' we ain't seen him since. 'E's a real scaredy cat, that Nautipus, I've always said it. By the way, Polly, nice outfit. Looks jus' loik peejamas.'

'They *are* pyjamas, Slugbucket,' laughed Polly.

'Oh, right,' said Slugbucket. 'Well, they're dead noice anyway.'

'So what's wrong with jus' leavin' 'em there?' he continued. 'What 'arm can they do under the floorboards?'

'None at all so long as they stay there,' replied the Captain. 'But if they can find their way down there they can find their way back up again. They could pop up right in the middle of Mr Tutt's inspection – or at any other time, come to that – and we can't have snakes running around the place, can we?'

'Slithering,' corrected Polly with a grin. The Captain laughed.

Yet still there was no solution in sight.

Eventually Polly decided that there was only one thing to do.

'I'll go down there,' she said.

Into the Darkness

The others stared at her.

'I'm small enough,' she persisted. 'And if I put the bee-keeping suit on, I'll be perfectly safe.'

'No, Polly,' said the Captain firmly. 'I couldn't let you do that. I think the best thing we can do for now is seal up the holes so they can't get out. Then as soon as Mr Tutt's gone we'll take up all the floorboards and get rid of them.'

'But we won't know for sure that we've found all the holes,' said Polly.

'Polly's right,' said Seymour. 'These floorboards are so gappy that they could probably squeeze in and out almost anywhere.'

But the Captain had made his decision and was already climbing out of his bee-keeping suit: there would be no more snake-catching until after the inspection. Polly knew better than to try changing the Captain's mind, but she also knew that unless those snakes were caught, there would always be a risk that Mr Tutt might discover them – and then what? The Captain ushered everyone into the corridor and closed the door securely behind them. Then he asked Slugbucket to take the most recently captured snake to the far corner of the woods and release it with the others. He and Seymour would gather the tools and materials they needed to seal up the holes in the floor. Polly, he suggested, could go back upstairs and continue her recuperation. There was nothing more she could do.

So the snake-catchers went their separate ways. Except that Polly didn't go very far. As soon as the others were out of sight, she turned around and let herself back into the kitchen. She headed straight for the cutlery drawer and picked out the heaviest, sturdiest knife she could find. Then she went to the larder and returned carrying a wire-mesh cage. Normally the Captain used it to stop bluebottles from landing on his cakes, but today Polly thought it would make a perfect snake trap. She put both pieces of equipment down on the kitchen table, then climbed into the Captain's bee-keeping suit. It was enormous. The sleeves hung down to the floor, so she rolled them up until her hands reappeared. Then she put on the gloves. These were also too big, but the elastic round the wrists kept them on tight, so that nothing would be able to slither up her sleeves. The trouser legs trailed along the floor behind her, so she tied a knot in the end of each one – she wouldn't need boots where she was going – and tried on the hood. The netting veil was difficult to see through at the best of times. Polly now realised that in the darkness under the floorboards it would be impossible, so she took it off again. Then she noticed Seymour's special work hat. He'd obviously been using the torch and the magnifying glass to search inside cupboards. Perfect. It didn't fit her at first, but she padded it out with a tea-towel until it fitted snugly. The spotlight on the end of the hat's left-hand stalk would light her way and allow her to use both hands to trap the snakes. And the magnifying glass on the other stalk? Well, it might come in handy.

When she had finished putting on her kit, she picked up the knife and pushed it between the ends of two floorboards. Firmly but gently, she tried to lever one up. At first it looked as if the knife might snap, but then she heard the tiny squeak of a nail shifting towards her. After a few attempts, the end of the floorboard lifted up just enough for her to squeeze her fingers underneath it. Then, with one prolonged pull the nails creaked free from the joist below and the floorboard lifted up.

Polly knelt down and lowered her head into the hole. She would just fit. A gap of about a foot separated the floorboards from the concrete foundations below. Several wooden cross-joists supported the floor and divided the space underneath into sections. Luckily, a narrow gap in each joist would allow Polly to move between them. She could see a dozen thin shafts of light, which shone down like knife blades through tiny holes and gaps in the floor, illuminating the clouds of dust and debris which floated through them. She guessed that most of them would be wide enough for a snake to escape through. All the more reason to trap them before they decided to go for an outing up Mr Tutt's trouser leg. Polly switched on the hat's spotlight and crawled into the hole, moving the loose floorboard back into its original position on top of her. For a second she felt a breath of panic at the thought that she might be sealing herself into her own coffin. But she reminded herself that she could push the floorboard back up any time she liked. It wasn't as if it was nailed down any more.

Pushing the cage along in front of her, she started to crawl forwards. She decided to head straight for the left-hand corner, which she thought would be the most likely place to find the snakes, as it was near the cupboard where the Captain had reported seeing holes in the floor. It was also the easiest corner to reach because there were no cross-joists blocking her way. But progress was still slow. She had to crawl almost flat on her stomach, wriggling from side to side like the snakes she was trying to catch. And the bee-keeping suit had a nasty habit of catching on splinters. Several times she had to go into reverse to unhook herself.

Eventually she was close enough to aim the spotlight directly into the corner. It was empty. That whole section was empty. There was nothing for it – she would have to work her way to the other side of the kitchen, squeezing through gaps in the supporting joists and checking each section as she went. Pushing the cage ahead of her, just in case there was a nasty surprise waiting there for her, she inched into the next section. Turning her head left and right, she discovered that her eyes had become so accustomed to the light that she could see to both ends. Apart from a few worryingly large cobwebs and lots of dust, the section was empty, so she crawled towards the gap in the next joist, which was a few feet away. A quick glance left and right showed her that this section too was empty. As was the next section. And the next. And the next.

Finally she approached the last section. The gap looked very small, but she knew the snakes had to be in there somewhere. She couldn't give up now. She took a deep breath and pushed the cage through the gap, then started to squeeze her head and shoulders in after it. When she was half-way through, the snakes attacked the cage with electric ferocity. The sudden jolt made Polly bang her head on the floorboard above, pushing the magnifying glass on Seymour's hat down in front of her face. When she looked up she saw the snakes at four times their actual size: 'Aaaargh!' Quickly she pushed the magnifying glass out of the way, then looked again – to see that there were two small snakes on the other side of the cage, lunging at it repeatedly. She knew she would have to capture them together, so she decided to wait for the next strike and then make her move. She didn't have to wait long. She could see one of the snakes already rearing up. A moment later it lunged and struck the cage hard, but this time Polly pushed after it, and just as it rejoined its companion she stretched out and flipped the cage over them. Bullseye. Polly watched as the two snakes struck out inside the cage, but they couldn't escape. She'd caught them.

A wave of relief washed over Polly, but no sooner had she started to bask in her success than her celebrations were cut short by the sound of footsteps. Two people had walked into the kitchen and had begun talking to each other just inches above her head. Fizzlesticks! she thought. She lay still and listened, but their voices were muffled by the floorboards, as if they were talking with woolly socks stuffed in their mouths. She could only guess who they might be. Surely it was too early for Mr Tutt to be there? Then again, perhaps he'd arrived early to catch them out. That was just the sort of thing inspectors did, wasn't it?

She turned herself around and, as quietly as she could, began to swivel and twist her way through the gaps in the joists towards her starting point. Every few seconds she would stop and listen. The voices were still there, and their owners were still moving to and fro across the floorboards, sending small clouds of dust down to settle in Polly's hair. Finally, as she crawled through the last gap, she began to make out a thin rectangular halo of light surrounding the loose floorboard. Good, they hadn't found it. All she had to do was crawl underneath and get ready to push as soon as the coast was clear. She would be up and out of there in seconds. She positioned herself under the floorboard and twisted herself on to her back ready to go. Now she just had to wait.

The muffled voices were right overhead again, but still she couldn't be certain who they belonged to. She would have to assume that one of them was Mr Tutt and stay put. For the first time she began to feel really frightened. She was hot and sticky, and the air was now so thick with dust that she was finding it hard to breathe. And because the floorboard was just an inch or two away from her face, she felt closed in, like a butterfly trapped in a matchbox. Then the voices stopped. She held her breath and listened. Still nothing. This was her chance. She knew she had to move quickly – she placed her hands on the underside of the floorboard, ready to push. But before she could, the whole floorboard seemed to explode as a pair of heavy boots stamped it back into position, driving the nails deep into the wooden joists with an enormous crack, and sending an avalanche of choking dust and debris cascading into Polly's face. It stung her eyes and filled her mouth, tickling the back of her throat like a million microscopic feathers. And then it happened. Before she had time to do anything about it, she coughed. Just a small one – surely no one would have heard it?

She held her breath once again and listened. All she could hear was her own heartbeat. Good. Perhaps with a monumental effort she could still escape. She counted silently to three . . . and pushed as hard as she could. The floorboard didn't budge. It didn't so much as creak. Its nails had been driven so firmly into the joists that an elephant might just as well have been sitting on it.

Suddenly Polly felt as if she'd been buried alive. Puffing her cheeks out, she pushed again and still nothing happened. Then again. And again. Exhausted and sobbing, she tried to gulp down clean air. But there was none to be had. Only dry, suffocating dust. She could feel herself about to cry out. She knew she couldn't. If Mr Tutt discovered her, all would be lost, and it would have been her fault. But the panic welling up inside her had a mind of its own. She could feel it expanding like a red-hot balloon, and any second it was going to burst out of her in an uncontrollable frenzy of kicking and screaming. And then she saw it. The tip of a knife, pushed through a crack just inches above her face. The blade slid slowly towards her and came to rest half an inch away from her nose. She watched in cross-eyed horror as it started to work its way backwards and forwards. Then a sliver of light appeared along the edge of the floorboard, and the nails started to groan as they were levered back out of the joist. She'd been caught after all.

As the floorboard lifted up, the light from the kitchen flooded into the gap and blinded her. She closed her eyes and surrendered herself, trembling, to the pair of hands which pulled her up into a sitting position. When she opened them she found Tom staring at her in disbelief.

'I saw Seymour's lamp shining through the crack

in the floorboards,' he explained. 'Come on, Mr Tutt will be here in a minute – the Captain's gone to get him.'

Tom helped Polly out of the hole and put the floorboard back into position before returning Seymour's work hat to the shelf. Then, as Polly seemed so wobbly on her feet, Tom carried her over his shoulder all the way to her room. As soon as they were inside, she started to tell him, in heaving, gulpy breaths, what had happened. He already knew some of it. He'd arrived early to find Mr Tutt at the gates scribbling notes on his clipboard. He had raced down through Beastlybark Wood to warn the Captain and caught up with him just as he was going into the kitchen with a bucket of wood-filler.

'He told me about the snakes,' Tom told her. 'And then, on his way out of the kitchen to find Mr Tutt, he saw the loose floorboard and jumped on it. That's when I heard you cough.'

By now, Polly had taken off the bee-keeping suit and was washing her hands and face in the sink. The Fizzle dissolved the dirt and grime instantly, and as soon as she cupped her hands and drank some from the tap she seemed, remarkably, to return to her old self.

'I found the missing snakes,' she announced proudly as she turned back to face him. 'There were two of them. I've got them trapped under the Captain's cake basket. They'll be safe there until Mr Tutt goes, and then the Captain will find them as soon as he takes up the floorboards.'

'Won't he think it's a bit odd that they're inside a cake basket?' asked Tom.

'I won't tell if you don't,' she grinned. 'Now shall we go back? I can't wait to see what Mr Tutt thinks of our shiny new kitchen.'

Polly left the bee-keeping suit to soak in a sinkful of Fizzle, then she and Tom went back downstairs. As they walked into the kitchen, the Captain looked up and greeted them. Mr Tutt, who was standing beside him, continued to look down at his notes. It was a good job he did too, because dangling like a noose from a roof beam right in front of him was a long green grass snake. Snake number six.

Of course, thought Polly miserably, we forgot to look up there.

As soon as Mr Tutt finished writing he would look up and see the snake, so Polly tried to signal to the Captain, using a series of frantic hand gestures and eye movements. Tom joined in and eventually – after making a few hand signals back to them, thinking it was some new kind of game they'd invented – the Captain understood and looked over to see the snake for himself. But it was too late. There was no time to distract Mr Tutt. He had dotted his last i and crossed his last t and was about to look up. Which he did. But instead of looking straight ahead, he looked behind him, as a large drop of Fizzle chose that precise moment to plop into the sink. This was no ordinary plop, though. It sounded as if a pebble had been dropped on to a big bass drum from the top of a tall building. It was a super-atomic-mega-plop, and it echoed backwards and forwards across the kitchen for several seconds, as if it had no intention of ever leaving the room. By the time Polly and Tom looked back towards Mr Tutt, the snake had vanished.

'I'd get that fixed if I were you,' advised Mr Tutt, nodding towards the tap before leaving the kitchen for the next part of his inspection. The Captain sneaked a wink at Polly and Tom as he followed Mr Tutt out of the door.

Polly and Tom decided there was nothing more they could do, so they settled down to wait for the Captain to return. Polly sat at the table and Tom went over to see if he could fix the dripping tap. He examined it carefully and tested it several times. Strangely, he could find nothing wrong with it. He even tried to make it drip again, but without success.

'That's because it was magic,' insisted Polly. 'The Fizzle forced its way out of the tap just to save us, don't you see?'

Tom turned to her. 'Polly, you know I think all that stuff about magic is nonsense. It was just luck, that's all.'

Polly huffed and crossed her arms, while Tom turned back to the sink to pour two glasses of Fizzle, which he carried to the table.

She watched him intently as he took his first sip. She wasn't to be deterred.

'So have you "Got the Fizzle" yet?' she asked him.

He smiled at her persistence. 'No, not yet, Polly. Sorry.'

'Never mind, you will,' she replied confidently.

They drank the rest of their Fizzle in silence and waited. Every few minutes someone would stick their head round the door and ask if there was any news, but the Captain was still with Mr Tutt. Then they would wait some more, listening to the kitchen clock ticking. Finally, after an hour which seemed more like two, the Captain returned. He shut the door behind him and leaned against it with his head back and his eyes shut. After taking a long deep breath he popped open a big beady eye and aimed it down at Polly.

'Would you mind passing me the washing up gloves, please, Polly?' he asked.

She fetched them and he put them on. Slowly, he dipped the tips of his fingers into his beard, like a surgeon about to perform a very delicate operation. After a moment he found what he was looking for – and very slowly and carefully pulled the sixth and last grass snake out by its tail.

'I would have put it in one of my pockets, but they were all full,' he explained, and with a little shiver dropped the snake into the nearest saucepan and replaced the lid.

'Now I suppose you'd like to know the result,' he said.

Open for Business

'Passed? PASSED?' Venetia Pike was livid with rage. 'You mean you didn't find *anything* wrong with the place at all? Did you check everything, Mr Tutt?'

'Everything,' he replied.

'Even the jars on the shelves in the kitchen?' she continued.

'Everything,' repeated Mr Tutt.

'Including the blue flour tin?' she persisted.

Mr Tutt was beginning to feel insulted.

'*Everything*,' he insisted indignantly. '*AS ALWAYS.*'

'It's all in my report,' he added, placing the document on the desk in front of her. 'In fact,' he continued, warming to the subject, 'they were fully compliant. I was particularly impressed with reference to By-Law 37, Subsection 29, Paragraph 1 of the 1947 Restaurant Utilities Workspace Act.'

Pike bristled. 'Speak English, Mr Tutt,' she snapped.

'The kitchen was spotless,' he explained. 'I've told Captain Shipley that he can resume business and that no new Council inspections will be required for at least five years. In fact, Mrs Tutt and I thought we might join Shipley Manor Country Club ourselves.'

He left the room. Venetia Pike stared down at his report in disgust. All the effort she'd put in. All that dressing up and trudging round in those revolting open-toed sandals. And this was the result: 'Fully Compliant'.

'I'll give you "Fully Compliant",' she snarled, and she picked up Mr Tutt's report and thrashed it wildly against the top of her computer until it was no more than a handful of torn and tattered shreds. Falling back into her chair exhausted, she tossed its remains into the waste paper basket.

'Do You Want To Quit?' asked the computer.

'I haven't even sssstarted yet,' Pike hissed as she ripped the computer's plug out of the wall.

Back at Shipley Manor the atmosphere was altogether jollier. The day after Mr Tutt's inspection the Captain pulled up the kitchen floorboards one by one. When eventually he found the cake basket – which to Polly's huge relief still contained the two snakes – he didn't appear to be in the least bit puzzled. In fact, he seemed delighted.

'Splendid,' he said. 'I was thinking of baking a special cake to celebrate anyway.'

And that was it. A few hours later the snakes were exploring their new home in the woods, the floorboards were back in position and the residents of Shipley Manor, plus Tom, were gathered round the kitchen table, tucking into a huge chocolate cake and discussing the future of Shipley Manor Country Club.

There was a lot to talk about. Passing Mr Tutt's inspection only solved the first of their problems. Now that they had been given permission to reopen, they had a second challenge to worry about: how to repay the money they'd borrowed from Mr Grub. They would have to attract hundreds of new members, each willing to pay for the privilege of exploring the Beastlybark Trail, staying in the cabins, swimming in the moat and drinking Fizzle in the Captain's Cocktail Lounge. And they had to do it quickly too, because they had barely enough money left to make their first monthly repayment to the bank.

'An' what 'appens if we don't 'ave enough money to pay the bank after that?' Slugbucket asked.

The Captain looked rather sheepish.

'Well, I must confess I'm not quite sure,' he admitted. 'You know, I've been so busy with the renovations and everything else that I haven't had time to read the loan contract yet. BUT,' he added confidently, prodding the table with his finger, 'Mr Grub assured me that there was nothing in the contract to worry about. Those were his exact words.'

No one around the table felt entirely comforted by this, least of all Tom. He knew that you should always read something properly before agreeing to it. Perhaps he should offer to take the contract home so that his father could look at it . . .? Soon, though, the conversation turned towards attracting new members. How would they do it?

'Got it!' Slugbucket shot one of his huge callused hands into the air. 'We could 'old the world's first Slug Olympics. The kids'd love it.'

There was a pause as everyone tried to imagine slugs pole-vaulting and jumping over hurdles.

'Nice idea, shipmate,' said the Captain. 'But I'm not sure everyone has a month to spare to watch the hundred-metre sprint.'

'Pity,' Slugbucket replied, slightly deflated. 'Some of 'em could do with a bit of a workout.'

'Call me old-fashioned, dear,' said Constance from her chair, 'but I don't think you can do better than a traditional Country Fayre.'

'It's certainly a possibility, Constance,' the Captain conceded. 'But with the special Shipley Manor touch. We could have raft races round the moat, exotic foodstalls –'

'An arts and crafts section, where visitors can make their own paintings to take home –' added Maggie.

'Plenty of foot-tapping music,' said Edna.

'And lots of entertainment for the children,' said Seymour. 'Like –'

'Slug races?' asked Slugbucket hopefully.

'– like Fizzlefish-catching competitions,' Seymour continued, 'and a knobbly knees contest.'

All eyes swivelled back to the Captain, whose knees were by far the knobbliest.

'Polly and Tom, what do you think?' he asked, blushing.

Polly, who so far had been stifling a yawn, knew exactly what she would do.

'Well, I think we should spend every penny we have left on a fantastic firework display, and invite everyone in Shipley to watch it for free,' she said confidently. 'That way thousands of people will turn up and see how wonderful it is here. I expect they'll all want to join Shipley Manor Country Club straight away.'

'Even if they don't,' Tom added more sensibly, despite feeling a tingle of excitement at Polly's idea, 'they'll still be hungry and thirsty, so you should sell enough food and drink to cover the cost of the fireworks anyway.'

The room fell silent as everyone considered Polly's suggestion. Then they burst into loud, whooping applause. It was a brilliant idea. A bit risky, to be sure, particularly if the weather turned out to be awful, but everyone felt certain that if it worked, their troubles could be over once and for all. So it was agreed. Shipley Manor would hold the biggest and best firework display the town had ever seen. It would be a night the people of Shipley would never forget, and to make sure that everybody came they would place a large advertisement in the following week's *Shipley Gazette*. Tom, for his part, would put posters up around the town and tell everyone he knew about the great event, beginning with his father.

Grand
Firework Spectacular

Watch the night sky explode into
life as we celebrate the reopening
of Shipley Manor Country Club
Saturday at 8 o'clock

Admission FREE

Venetia Pike sat stiff and upright in her office chair, motionless except for her narrow, slightly bloodshot eyes, which darted left and right on the trail of a large bluebottle which had made the fatal mistake of entering her office uninvited. She held a rolled-up copy of the *Shipley Gazette* high above her head, like an executioner's axe waiting to fall. The moment the fly landed on the telephone in front of her, the axe flashed down with the finely judged force of a seasoned executioner – hard and fast enough to kill, soft enough not to make a mess. Smiling with satisfaction, Pike flicked the dead fly into the palm of her hand and lifted it up to her face.

'Next time, make an appointment,' she said sharply. Then she dropped it into her jacket pocket – a little treat for Viceroy to enjoy later – and picked up the phone to call her business partner.

'Greasy little man,' she muttered under her breath as she dialled Grub's number. 'Baaarclay daaaarling, it's fluffy bunny here,' she purred, twisting the telephone cord around her little finger (just as she did Grub). 'There's an advert in today's *Gazette* which I thought you might find in-ter-est-ing.'

She could hear his heavy breathing at the other end of the phone. Just the sound of it turned her stomach.

'You mean the firework display at Shipley Manor, sweet pea?' he wheezed. 'I heard about it this morning. That idiot Sterling was in here wittering on about how spectacular it was going to be. Apparently, our friend Captain Shipley has decided to spend every last penny on it.'

'Exccccellent,' said Pike. 'So he'll have absolutely nothing left when you turn up to demand all the money back.'

'Well, he *might*, my little sponge-cake,' Grub continued, worryingly. 'That's the thing. They're hoping that on the night, half the town will decide to join Shipley Manor Country Club and pay to become members there and then. I doubt if they'll make enough to pay off the whole loan, but this firework display is certainly their only hope.'

'Howww fassscinating,' she replied. 'So it would probably be rather a sssshame if the whole evening was a bit of a . . . *wash-out* then, wouldn't it?'

After a moment's hesitation, Grub caught up with her.

'Ohhh, I see . . . absolutely, sugar-plum,' he agreed. 'I mean, who in their right mind would join a country club that was so *wet* that it couldn't even organise a simple firework display?'

'And if the story was *ssssplashed* all over the newspapers –' she added.

'Everyone for miles around would know about it – they'd be a complete laughing stock,' he agreed.

'A laughing stock with no members and no money left –' she prompted him.

'– to repay the loan to the bank!' he continued triumphantly, as if he had just solved a long and complicated puzzle.

Pike lifted her eyes to the ceiling.

'Precccccisely,' she said. 'So perhaps you and I should give them a little help preparing their fireworks – put the *dampeners* on the event, so to speak.'

Grub looked down at the glass of water on his desk.

'Oh, ab-so-lutely, ducky love,' he said. 'After all, helping local businesses is what we're here for, isn't it? It's our Official Duty.'

Grub so enjoyed these conversations with Pike. They confirmed what he already knew, that he and Venetia were meant for each other. They shared the same ideas, the same dreams, even the same secrets. A perfect couple, or so he thought. (Pike knew different, of course. Because as soon as the Shipley Manor Housing Estate – or whatever it was she decided to turn the place into – had made her rich, she would see to it that Grub never clapped his little piggy eyes on her again.)

When they'd finished talking, Grub sank back into his chair and clasped his hands behind his head. He imagined the front page of the following week's *Shipley Gazette*: 'FIREWORKS FIZZLE OUT'. It wouldn't be long now before the Captain and Shipley Manor Country Club were completely finished. Then he and Venetia could enjoy tea and scones on the balcony at Shipley Manor. Lord and Lady Grub. He could almost taste the jam.

Later that day, much to Tom and his dad's surprise, Grub offered to put one of the posters in the front window of Shipley Bank. He even took it upon himself to call the *Shipley Gazette* and suggest that a newspaper reporter should go along to record the event. Tom had also been allowed to pin posters up at school and inside the library and several shops, so that by the end of the week almost everyone in Shipley knew about the forthcoming firework display. And as far as Tom could tell from talking to the other boys at school, most of them were planning to go. Everything seemed to be going according to plan.

Tom's Confession

The Friday before the big firework display, Tom finished school and headed straight for Shipley Manor to help with the preparations. The Captain had asked him to work as many hours as possible, so tucked under his arm was a sleeping bag that would enable him to stay overnight. The first thing he noticed as he rounded the bend in the drive was a bonfire the size of a small cottage. It stood in the field directly below the garden terrace and was built from all the old wood left over from the Great Storm – what better way to use it up after all these years than to help relaunch Shipley Manor Country Club? An area in front of the bonfire had been roped off for the fireworks and, running across it towards him, her hair an explosion of colour and with a dozen long silver ribbons trailing behind her in the wind, was a very excited-looking Polly.

I might have known it, thought Tom. She's dressed as a firework.

She caught up with him at the bottom of the drive.

'Come and look at this,' she said breathlessly, taking his hand and leading him up the short track towards Slugbucket's main tool shed. Polly threw its door open.

'Look at that lot,' she said proudly.

Tom peered inside to find the biggest collection of fireworks he had ever seen – stacked to the ceiling in dozens of brightly coloured boxes. The names of the fireworks, stencilled on to each box in large bold letters, described the fantastic visual effects that would be experienced by the people of Shipley the following night: Monster Starbursts, Giant Comets, Wriggling Screechers, Crackling Demons and Dazzling Sky Poppers. And alongside the boxes in three metal dustbins, several dozen huge rockets stood to attention like soldiers, eye to eye with Tom. He tilted his head over to one side and began reading the names on each rocket: Triple Blaster, Flashing Thunder, Red Devil, King Slayer.

Wow, he thought. This is going to be good.

Suddenly the light dimmed as a tall figure stepped into the doorway.

'Now you mind yerselves,' said Slugbucket. 'One spark an' this lot'll blow sky 'igh. I'm lockin' 'em up for the night now, so let's be 'avin' yer.'

Tom took one last look, then he and Polly watched as Slugbucket closed the door behind them and secured it with a hefty padlock.

'Should be quite summat when that lot goes up, I reckon,' he said. 'Now, Tom, be you ready for some 'ard work? The Captain's wantin' to get loads done tonight so we don't 'ave any last-minute panics tomorrow.'

Tom nodded eagerly. 'Very sensible,' he said.

'Well then,' said Slugbucket, 'I reckons the most important thing to do is to get up on that shed roof and check for any damage – any tears in the felt where the rain might get in. Whatever 'appens, these fireworks 'ave got to stay bone-dry till we lets 'em off tomorrow. If you sees anything needs fixin', jus' do it like you did with 'em cabins. The toolbox is in there,' he said, nodding towards his caravan. 'I'm sure Polly will 'elp you, won't you, Polly?'

Polly nodded. She loved climbing and was already standing on one of the caravan's wheels, preparing to hoist herself up on to the shed roof. She clambered up and Tom followed behind her. As soon as they were up there they could tell that the roof was in perfect condition. Nevertheless, they took their time examining it, using the opportunity to look around the estate and see what everyone else was doing.

After leaving Polly and Tom, Slugbucket had gone into the woods to fetch a huge tree-trunk to add to the bonfire. From the roof they could now see him driving the digger down the hill, the gnarled old trunk clamped between its metal jaws like a bone between the teeth of a giant mechanical dog. They also spotted Seymour as he made his way up towards the main gates, checking each of the lamps that would, the following night, illuminate the driveway like an airport runway and guide their visitors safely down to the house. And at the bottom of the driveway they could see Maggie inside one of the treadmills, enjoying an evening stroll with Calypso over her shoulder. Polly's mother did this every day. As well as keeping the electricity generator topped up, the slow, rhythmic creaking of the wheel never failed to send the baby off to sleep. The Captain and the others, Polly and Tom knew, were busy preparing food for the following day, so when they'd finished on the roof they jumped down and headed towards the kitchen.

The Captain turned round from the cooker to greet them.

'Tom,' he beamed, 'has Polly shown you the fireworks yet?'

'They look fantastic,' said Tom.

The Captain's eyes lit up. 'Do you really think so?' he said. 'Oh good – Shipley Manor's future is relying on them. Now,' he added, 'we've got hundreds of empty bottles in the cellar that need filling up with Fizzle – you and Polly can make a start on that if you like.'

Then he turned back to the cooker just in time to stop a saucepan from boiling over.

'I've never been down there before,' said Tom, as he and Polly headed to the cellar. 'Where's the door?'

'It's invisible,' she replied.

'Oh, I see,' he said, laughing. 'So it's a magic door then, is it?'

'Of course,' said Polly a little indignantly. 'What else would you call an invisible door?'

'Well hidden,' he answered, grinning from ear to ear.

Polly narrowed her eyes at him.

'Anyway,' she continued suddenly, 'I bet you can't guess *why* it's invisible.'

Tom thought hard. Why would an old house like Shipley Manor have a hidden doorway? Proper, sensible historical reasons, of course. Could it be that the Captain's seafaring ancestors were smugglers and needed a place to hide their smuggled goods? Or maybe they needed somewhere to hide from invaders in times of war? Perhaps the door led to a secret escape tunnel, which surfaced somewhere up in the woods or even down by the sea – inside a cave perhaps. He tried them all out on Polly.

'No, none of those,' she said eventually. 'Do you give in?'

'Go on then, tell me.'

'The Captain wallpapered over the door by mistake,' she laughed.

Tom smiled and shook his head. He should have known.

Polly continued, 'After he'd done it, he said that every old house should have at least one secret door and that the cellar door could be ours. So instead of peeling the wallpaper off, he cut a slit round it and it's been like that ever since. Have you spotted it yet?'

Tom looked down the corridor. He couldn't see any door.

'It's best if you close your eyes and run your fingers along the wall,' Polly suggested.

So, feeling a bit silly, he followed her advice and half-way along the corridor he felt a slight ridge in the wallpaper. He opened his eyes and saw a thin, straight crack leading up from the floor. Then another one across the top and another one coming down again. He'd found it. Polly joined him and tapped the door with her fist. It sprang open, and a small light came on inside the doorway.

'I'll go first,' she said, squeezing past him.

When they reached the bottom of the steps, Polly ran her fingers along a row of switches as if she was a concert pianist, and section by section the cellar flickered into life. The part of the cellar in which they were now standing was cavernous. It covered most of the area beneath the main house and reminded Tom of an underground car park. Every few yards stone pillars rose out of the concrete floor and splayed out like hands to support the weight of the house above. These pillars were evenly spaced around a much larger column which squatted in the centre like an enormous tree-trunk. This was the base of the Crow's Nest. Around it, the high ceiling supported a network of criss-crossed pipes and cables which carried Fizzle and electricity to the house above and, in the case of blowpipe messages, up through the main column to the top of the Crow's Nest. Then Tom noticed two small arches leading through into separate rooms at each end of the cellar. One of these, he guessed correctly, was the generator room, where power from the treadmills was converted into electricity. This is where Polly took him first.

'The Captain calls it the Engine Room,' she explained. 'Just like on a real ship.'

Inside, Tom could see two huge springs. Each was connected at the top to a series of cogs and pulleys which led through the thick stone walls to the treadmills outside. At the bottom, more cogs and pulleys connected the springs to an electricity generator, from which two levers – one to control each spring – protruded like a pair of metal rabbit's ears. The principle was simple. Turning the treadmills outside compressed the springs. When a lever was switched to the ON position, coiled-up power was released from the bottom of the spring into the generator, where it was turned into electricity. If the lever was set to OFF, the spring would store up its power until it was needed. But there was also a third setting: REVERSE.

'What happens if you switch the lever to REVERSE?' asked Tom.

'I don't think anyone's ever tried that before,' admitted Polly, 'but I suppose it would just do what it says and send the power back to where it came from – back into the treadmills.'

'So do you think they'd start turning round by themselves, then?' asked Tom.

'Probably,' she replied, smiling. 'Like magic.'

Tom noticed that the mechanism above one of the springs was in motion, which meant that Maggie was still turning the treadmill outside. It reminded him that there was work to be done.

'So where are all these bottles, then?' he asked.

Polly took Tom to the other end of the cellar and led him through the second archway into a store room.

'There they are,' she said, pointing to the far wall. Stacked against it were hundreds of brightly coloured crates, which rose to the ceiling in uneven towers, like a baby giant's building bricks. In each crate, a dozen empty Fizzle bottles sat expectantly, waiting to be filled.

'No wonder the Captain wanted me to stay the night,' said Tom. 'This is going to take ages.'

An old worktop with a sink in the middle stretched along another wall, and next to it a small doorway led from the store room into the Captain's Cocktail Lounge.

'Is that door invisible on the other side too?' asked Tom.

'Of course it is,' Polly replied. 'What would be the point in only one of the cellar doors being hidden?'

She went through the door to collect a couple of bar stools and by the time she returned two crates were ready and waiting on the worktop. Polly turned on the tap.

'Last one to a hundred's a sea slug,' she said.

A thousand bottles later they emerged from the cellar to a dark and silent house. They had completely lost track of time and realised that everyone else had gone to bed. Tired and hungry, they crept into the kitchen and turned on the light. The clock told them it was past midnight.

'Flour tin?' yawned Tom.

'Ha, ha,' replied Polly. 'You can have a biscuit if you like – I'm going to make myself a sandwich. I'll make you one as well if you ask me nicely.'

A few minutes later they had prepared a delicious midnight feast. Polly suggested that they took it to her perch in the woods, so Tom gathered up his sleeping bag and together they tiptoed out of the house.

'Are you sure it's all right to do this?' he asked, half-way over the drawbridge. 'Shouldn't we ask permission, or tell them where we're going or something?'

'Don't be such an old fusspot, Tom. I do this all the time,' Polly replied. 'Anyway, I expect they're all asleep or busy with Calypso. Now come on, I'm hungry.'

Half-way up the track they passed Slugbucket's caravan. His orange bucket was on the doorstep, which meant that he was inside. Sure enough, as they drew closer they could hear him snoring like one of his chainsaws.

'It's just as well he sleeps out here,' Polly whispered, 'otherwise we'd all have to wear earplugs.'

At the top of the track, Polly handed the picnic basket to Tom and climbed the tree which marked the start of the Beastlybark Trail. She seemed to climb it effortlessly, and on closer inspection Tom noticed that small climbing pegs had been knocked into the trunk. He was wondering how he was going to climb the tree with both hands full when the hooked end of a Fizzlestick appeared in front of him.

'Hang everything on the end, Tom,' a voice whispered down to him. 'Then you can climb up.'

Tom hooked the picnic basket and his sleeping bag on to the end of the stick, then Polly lifted it back up into the tree. Tom climbed after it. Soon he found himself standing on Polly's Perch. Polly had laid out the sleeping bag for them to sit on and was busy unpacking the food. Tom looked around. Above him, through a gap in the tree, he could see the night sky. In front, the dark shadow of the house was surrounded by a glittering halo, as the moonlight danced on the surface of the moat.

'We could go for a swim in the moat later if you like,' Polly said.

Tom dismissed the idea. 'It's much too late.'

'No, it's not. Says who?' said Polly.

'Everyone knows you shouldn't go swimming in the dark,' he told her.

'It's not dark at all,' she persisted. 'The moon's really bright.'

'Besides, the water will be too cold – we might get cramp.'

'Actually it's really warm, Tom. I dipped my finger in earlier. Come on, it'll be fun.'

'No, Polly, sorry.'

'But it's safe, Tom. Just for once stop being so sensible!'

'It's nothing to do with that,' he said quietly.

'Then what is it?' she persisted. 'Why don't you want to go for a swim?'

Tom shrugged his shoulders.

'Why not?' she repeated.

'Because I can't swim. All right?' he confessed finally.

There was a silence as Polly's jaw dropped open. She thought every boy his age knew how to swim.

'Why not?' she asked.

So he told her. As the two of them sat cross-legged and ate their picnic, Tom told Polly how his mother had drowned trying to save a rule-breaker.

He explained that for years afterwards he had refused to go anywhere near the sea, kicking and screaming at the very mention of it. Neither would he set foot inside the Shipley Swimming Baths, let alone take swimming lessons. Eventually his father had stopped trying to force him through the doors, hoping that one day Tom would decide for himself that it would be sensible to learn to swim.

'That's what Dad thinks everyone should be, you see – sensible,' Tom went on. 'He says that if we all stuck to the rules and did what's right all the time, then Mum would still be alive.'

'What she did was so brave, Tom,' Polly said.

Tom nodded. If only he was too. He didn't even have the courage to learn to swim.

'Do you remember her?' Polly asked him.

'Only a little,' Tom replied hesitantly – he wasn't used to people asking him about his mother. 'But I still miss her. I remember she was always picking me up and dancing around with me. Dad says that it didn't matter where we were – in a shop or walking down Shipley High Street – if Mum felt like dancing she'd just do it. Dad won't admit it, but I even remember him joining in sometimes.'

He smiled at her warmly.

'She was a bit like you, I suppose.'

Polly smiled back, then they fell into silence for a moment.

'I'm a very good paddler, though,' he joked.

Polly laughed. 'More cake?' she asked him.

'Got any water biscuits?' he replied, making her laugh again.

When they were full, they lay back with their hands cupped behind their heads, and imagined how the same night sky would look the following evening, as Shipley Manor celebrated its reopening in spectacular style.

'It'll be magic,' concluded Polly drowsily, moments before she fell asleep.

Let There Be Light

'You're late,' hissed Pike, stepping out into the moonlight from the shadow of the gatepost.

'I'm sorry, sweet pea,' Grub whispered back in a tiptoey sort of voice. 'It took me ages to find these.'

He was carrying a bucket in one hand and a pair of bolt-cutters in the other.

'What's that for?' asked Pike, nodding towards the bucket.

'Well,' Grub replied hesitantly, 'I thought we were – er, going to fill it up in the moat and empty it all over the fireworks. Make them unusable. That was the plan, wasn't it?'

'Whatever gave you that idea?' Pike answered with a thin smile. 'No, I have ssssomething far, far more sssspectacular in mind, Barclay. Come on.'

She led the way through the doorway into Shipley Manor Country Club. At the top of the driveway they cut down past the greenhouses and into the woods. Then they headed downhill towards the house. Even with help from a brightly moonlit sky, it was difficult to pick their way through the undergrowth. Progress was slow, and several times Pike's high heels were snared by fallen branches, causing her to lose her balance. This was wonderful for Grub, who bobbed along beside her like an over-affectionate puppy, steadying her and occasionally, joy of joys, catching his beloved Venetia in his arms. She, of course, hated every moment of it. She couldn't bear the little man and here he was grabbing her with his horrible sticky hands every time she tripped over a stupid twig. She vowed that at the earliest opportunity she would rip out every tree, every bush and every plant on the estate and build hundreds of expensive flats there instead. She would become so rich that she would never have to look at his sweaty, puffed-up face again. After a few minutes, much to Pike's relief, they were able to join the Beastlybark Trail, which provided a much easier route to the house. Pike was now able to stride out confidently. Unlike Grub, who had never seen the Beastlybark Trail before. He shuffled along nervously behind her, twitching this way and that at the gnarled and sinister faces which seemed to lurch out at him from every tree-trunk along the route. Pike wasn't impressed at all. The last thing she needed was a jumpy accomplice.

'Get a grip, man,' she snapped eventually. 'They're only made out of wood. WOOD! They're not going to come alive and eat you. Now come on.'

When they reached the bottom of the trail they crouched in the shadow of a large tree-trunk. From there a track led down to the main driveway, close to the house. To the right of the track, about half-way down, Slugbucket's caravan and the shed next to it sat bathed in moonlight.

'Right,' whispered Pike, 'from now on we'll have to be very quiet. That peculiar little girl told me during my Official Tour that the gardener – Slugbrain or something – lives in that caravan there. Now are you sure the fireworks are kept in the shed, Barclay?'

'Almost certain,' Grub replied. 'Sterling told me that the Captain planned to buy enough fireworks to fill the main tool shed. And that's it.'

'Excellent,' said Pike.

'So what's the plan, dearest heart?' whispered Grub.

'Well, you can forget that for a start,' she said, pointing to the bucket. 'You'd need an entire fire brigade to soak that many fireworks. Anyway, we can't let a shedload of perfectly good fireworks go to waste, can we? It's against Council policy. No, Barclay, we need to let these fireworks fulfil their destiny – we need to let them do what their maker intended.'

'You mean – ?'

Pike pulled out a box of matches.

'That's right,' she said. 'I think we should have a little firework spectacular of our own. Let's go.'

Like shadow puppets, the two silhouettes moved silently down the track in slow, deliberate steps, taking care to avoid any stone or twig that might make a noise. They paused behind Slugbucket's caravan and listened to him snoring.

No wonder they make him sleep out here, thought Pike. Satisfied that there was no one else around, they moved to the front of the shed. Pike rubbed the back of two bony fingers across the dusty window and peered inside. Then she turned to Grub and nodded. The fireworks were there, just as Sterling had said. Grub lifted the bolt-cutters to the padlock, but Pike put her hand on his arm to stop him. She raised a forefinger to her lips to remind Grub of the need for silence. Bolt-cutters would be too noisy. Besides, if the lock was broken the Captain would know that there had been intruders. She reached into her hair, pulled out a hairgrip and began to pick the lock. Grub gurgled with admiration as, a mere few seconds later, the padlock sprang open with a soft click. Pike handed it to him and eased open the door.

'Stay here and keep watch,' she whispered, before disappearing through the doorway. Once inside she took out a small pocket torch and looked around. The pile of firework boxes sat in the centre of the shed like an uneven cardboard pyramid. Pike stretched as far into the pile as she could and used her long razor-like thumbnail to slice open a large box labelled 'Starburst Surprise'.

Oh, it'll be a surprise all right, she thought as she removed one of the fireworks for closer examination. It was a cardboard tube about twice the height of a tin can and as heavy as a bag of sugar. A length of blue touch-paper protruded invitingly from one end. On the outside of the tube the end of the universe was depicted in a scene of cataclysmic cosmic destruction, as billions of stars burst into blinding, explosive oblivion.

Well now, my incendiary friend, she thought, I think you'll do very nicely.

She put it to one side, then took out six more, which she laid down on the box in front of her, arranged so that they were facing outwards like the spokes of a wheel, with the touch-papers meeting in the centre. She surrounded the wheel with packing material to keep it stable, then lifted other boxes and rockets into the direct line of fire around it. Next she ripped the touch-paper from the first firework and shook it upside down. The firework's contents sprayed out of the hole, coating the surrounding boxes in a fine layer of explosive powder. Finally, she took a tiny birthday candle from her pocket and, with a delicate twist, teased it into the centre of the wheel of fireworks she'd created, so that it was standing upright in a nest of blue touch-paper. She calculated that once she lit the candle the flame would take less than five minutes to burn down to the touch-paper and ignite the fireworks. Plenty of time for her and Grub to escape up the drive.

She stood back and admired her handiwork. There was only one thing left to do.

'Let there be light,' she whispered as she struck the match.

'– firework spectacular of our own. Let's go.'

That was all Polly heard. Or thought she'd heard. She had just woken up and couldn't decide whether the voice beneath the perch had been real or imaginary. It had seemed real enough, and somehow familiar too, even though it was barely a whisper. She looked at the moon. It had moved.

She and Tom must have been asleep for at least a couple of hours. She nudged Tom in the ribs, but he didn't wake up, so she rolled over on to her tummy and wriggled to the edge of the perch until she could peer over the side. There was no one there – at least, not any more. She closed her eyes and listened. Everything was quiet except for the occasional owl hoot and the sound of a distant chainsaw, which she knew to be Slugbucket enjoying his night's sleep. So what had the voice said? Something about the fireworks? Eventually she decided that even if she hadn't really heard a voice, even if she'd only dreamt she'd heard it, then it could still be some kind of premonition. Either way, she wouldn't be able to sleep a wink until she knew for sure that the fireworks were safe. She would have to go down to the shed to find out. Reluctantly, she picked up her Fizzlestick and lowered herself silently to the ground.

Polly crouched among the roots at the base of the tree – much as Pike and Grub had done just minutes earlier – and let her eyes follow the track down, looking for movement. Nothing. Next she followed the line of the driveway up from the house until it disappeared into the trees. That's when she saw them. Two shadowy figures running up the driveway, disappearing round the bend a heartbeat later. Then she knew. 'The fireworks!'

Polly leaped up and ran as fast as she could towards the shed. Half-way down she realised that there was something wrong with the shed window. It wasn't black. It was orange. Why was it orange? She raced on and flung herself against the window, pressing her face up against the glass to see inside. Then she gasped. Through a gap in the pile of firework boxes she saw the tiny birthday candle, flickering menacingly, polluting the inside of the shed with its sickly orange glow. And it had almost reached the touch-paper ranged around it. Polly pulled at the door but it was fastened tight with the padlock. Without thinking, she swung her Fizzlestick behind her head and brought it crashing down against the window. Shattered glass flew everywhere, but vicious shards still remained around the frame like sharks' teeth. She poked and prodded furiously until she'd knocked them out, then lifted herself up through the window, landing on her hands and rolling into a painful somersault on the other side.

It was only a few feet away now. An innocent little birthday candle, transformed into a monstrous tool of destruction. She had to put it out. She could see that only seconds remained before the flame reached the touch-paper. She knew that if she tried to shift any surrounding boxes out of the way the movement might unbalance the candle. And it was too far away to blow out. She would have to squeeze her body through the gap, far enough to reach out and snuff the flame out with her fingers. Ignoring the danger she was in, she lay on her side and started to inch her way between two of the boxes. She didn't take her eyes off the candle for one second. If she saw it tip over, she could at least make a desperate lunge for it. Then the gap narrowed. Without pushing the boxes aside she could go no further. Perhaps she could just reach. She licked her thumb and forefinger and stretched her arm out towards the flame. She was two inches short. Every muscle in her body strained and stretched as she tried to make herself just that little bit longer. One inch. Nearly there. She was so close. Then a tiny brown freckle appeared on the edge of one of the touch-papers and began to grow. Then another. Then – before Polly had time to see the freckle turn into a flame, two strong hands grabbed her ankles and dragged her backwards out of the gap, and pushed her head first through the open doorway. It was Tom. He threw himself on top of her a moment later, just as the first Starburst Surprise came spectacularly to life. Instantly it ignited the other Starbursts, which thumped and banged around the shed's insides, filling it with a whirling tornado of white hot sparks. These fell and settled on the other firework boxes, like burning ash thrown out of a volcano, and started to smoulder their way down through the cardboard to the fireworks inside. Once the chain reaction had begun, there was no stopping it. The rest of the fireworks soon joined the party and in a few seconds the shed had erupted in a multi-coloured frenzy of heat and light as Dazzling Sky Poppers, Crackling Demons, Killer Bees and Red Devil Rockets thundered around the shed in a terrifying display of explosive exhibitionism. Some escaped through the door, showering Polly and Tom with burning sparks as they whizzed and whooshed and screeched past them into the night. Others, like Firecrackers and Jumping Jacks, burst through the shed roof and popped and spattered like machine-gun fire around them. All they could do was keep their heads down and their ears covered. Like the people of Shipley, they missed a spectacular show.

Gradually, the noise started to subside. Tom reached out to retrieve the abandoned bolt-cutters – which he'd used to break the padlock and open the shed door – and, holding them at arm's length, pushed the door closed. Then he stood up and helped Polly to her feet. But before either of them could say anything, the shed burst into flames. Huge tongues of fire licked its walls and rose into the dark night sky. There was nothing Polly or Tom could do but watch in stunned silence. Then they realised that some of the flames were jumping sideways, over to Slugbucket's caravan. Surely the noise of the fireworks had woken him up? He couldn't possibly still be inside? Polly ran up the wooden steps to his door. It was locked, so she pressed the side of her head against it. She couldn't believe her ears. He was still fast asleep, snoring. Then she felt a sudden burst of heat on the back of her legs. She turned round and saw that the two wheels nearest the shed had caught fire. It would soon spread to the rest of the caravan. She hammered on the door and screamed Slugbucket's name, but he continued to snore. The bottom step caught fire just as Tom arrived with a bucket of water from the moat. He scored a direct hit, putting the step out in one go, but no sooner had he done that than the middle step caught alight.

'Get off the caravan, Polly!'

Polly ignored him and continued pounding hysterically on the door with her fist.

'Slugbucket, wake up!'

Finally the third step caught fire, and the sudden searing heat forced her flat against Slugbucket's door. Tom appeared on the other side of the caravan.

'You have to jump off, Polly,' he shouted to her. 'The wheels on this side are going to catch fire any second and then you'll be trapped.'

'But I can't leave Slugbucket!' Polly wailed, tears streaming down her face.

'You have to,' Tom shouted back. 'We'll push the caravan down the track into the moat – it's the only way.'

Polly nodded and took one last look at the door. She leaped to the ground just as the other cartwheels burst into flames. Tom was already at the rear of the caravan trying to move it. Polly joined him and threw herself at the task. Together, heads down, they inched the wheels forward. But they didn't get far. After a few feet one of the front wheels rolled into an empty puddle hole. Try as they might, they couldn't push it out the other side. They were losing valuable seconds. All the wheels were now well ablaze, as were the steps. It was only a matter of time before the flames engulfed the whole caravan and its lone sleeping occupant.

'Slugbucket!' screamed Polly, for what she feared might be the last time. 'Waaaake up!'

Frantically they started to rock the caravan backwards and forwards inside the puddle hole. If only they could clear this, it was a clear run down to the moat. Forwards, backwards, forwards, backwards, PUSH. They tried again. Forwards, backwards, forwards, backwards, PUSH. This time the wheel catapulted out of the puddle hole. Did *they* do that? Polly looked behind her. The Captain was there, reaching over their heads and heaving the caravan forwards with a look of grim determination on his face that she'd never seen before. Gradually, the speed of the caravan built up until they could no longer keep up with it. They let go and watched it hurtle down the track, its wheels ablaze and spinning like four giant Catherine wheels. When the track veered left to link up with the driveway, the caravan continued travelling straight, leaving the track and ploughing two parallel furrows through the rough grass down to the moat. Finally, it launched itself off the edge and landed with a huge, sizzling belly-flop in the water. The impact took it deep into the water, extinguishing all the flames, before it bounced back up to the surface. There it stayed, floating peacefully as if nothing had happened.

Polly ran to the water's edge and leaped on to the caravan, followed closely by Nautipus, who had appeared suddenly at her heels. She banged on the door.

'Slugbucket!' she shouted. 'Are you all right?'

This time the door creaked open and Slugbucket shuffled out into the moonlight. He rubbed his eyes and looked down at Polly. Then, because he couldn't quite believe what he was seeing, he rubbed them again. But Polly was still there, her arms and legs covered in cuts and bruises, her torn clothes peppered with burn holes and scorch marks, her face so blackened by smoke and dirt that she looked like a chimney sweep.

'Mornin', Polly,' he yawned. ''Ave oi missed summat?'

She launched herself forwards, almost knocking him over as she threw her arms around his waist. He put his arms around her too, then squinted over her head in the direction of the Captain and Tom, and at the shed, which was burning beyond salvation behind them. Finally, he looked around at the water which was gently lapping the sides of his caravan.

'Well, oi always fancied livin' on an 'ouseboat,' he said.

At that moment it started to rain – big, wet, dollopy rain, as if someone had turned on a giant tap. Considering that there had been a cloudless night sky only minutes before, this struck Tom as odd. Even odder was that it appeared to be raining on the shed and nowhere else. Tom looked up and saw that the water wasn't falling from the sky at all. Instead, it appeared to curve in a perfect arc from the top of the Crow's Nest. He stood and watched as the shed roof collapsed under the weight of the water and it poured inside, gradually subduing the flames and converting the shed and its contents to one soggy, steaming mess. Then it stopped. Polly jumped back on to the bank and rushed to the shed to retrieve her battle-scarred Fizzlestick from the wreckage. It was badly charred and the hook was still hot, but nevertheless it was still in one piece. She tucked it under her arm, then turned to Tom.

'You idiot!' she shouted.

'Pardon?' said Tom, hoping he'd misheard her.

'If you hadn't pulled me out of the shed, Mr Sensible, this would never have happened! I was nearly there, Tom – one more second and I'd have put the flame out. Now what are we going to do?'

Tom went weak at the knees. The thought that this whole terrible mess could be his fault made him feel sick. But he had done the right thing, hadn't he? Then again, everything here was so different from what he was used to, he wasn't sure any more. He'd woken up, he'd seen Polly running down the track, he'd chased after her and watched her go into the shed full of fireworks. Then he'd seen the flame through the window, and just knew that Polly wouldn't give a thought to the danger she was in. So he'd pulled her out. What else should he have done?

'Is that what happened, Tom? Did you pull Polly out of the shed?' the Captain asked him sternly.

Tom was too choked to answer. He had tears in his eyes and a lump in his throat the size of an orange. He just nodded.

The Captain looked hard at Polly, then stepped up to Tom and threw his arms around him, lifting him off the ground in a bear-hug so tight that it forced the air from Tom's lungs. Tom's body stiffened with embarrassment, his arms glued rigid to his sides, his bright red face unable to decide on an appropriate expression.

Finally the Captain released him.

'Thank you, Tom,' he said gratefully. 'Consider yourself promoted to First Mate.'

Then the Captain turned to Polly.

'I think you owe Tom an apology,' he said quietly, wagging his finger at the night sky. 'If it wasn't for his common sense and quick thinking, you could very well be scattered across the sky like those stars.'

Polly knew he was right, and hung her head in shame for a moment. Then she stepped over to Tom.

'Sorry, Tom,' she said sheepishly. 'Don't worry, I'm not going to hug you as well.'

The moment was interrupted as Seymour wheeled himself up the track in his pyjamas.

'Is the fire out?' he called as soon as he was within earshot. 'I can turn the Fizzle back on again if you like.'

'There's no need,' replied the Captain. 'How in the name of Neptune did you manage that, Seymour?'

'It's something I rigged up a few days ago. Tom suggested that if we were going to have a firework display, it might be sensible to have some kind of outside sprinkler system arranged in case of emergencies. It seemed like an excellent idea, so I invented a way of pumping Fizzle up the blowpipes and out through the loudspeakers at the top of the Crow's Nest. Instant rain, you might say.'

'Well, your aim's pretty good, Seymour – it landed right on target,' said the Captain.

'Oh, that had nothing to do with me,' Seymour replied. 'I haven't worked out how to aim it yet. The Fizzle did that all by itself.'

The Captain nodded as though Seymour's explanation made perfect sense.

'See!' said Polly, nudging Tom in the ribs. 'Fizzle to the rescue again.'

'A bit late, if you ask me,' he replied, glancing over at the smouldering heap that was once Slugbucket's shed.

Moments later Edna, Maggie and Calypso arrived. Maggie ran straight to Tom and thrust Calypso into his reluctant care, so that she could cradle

Polly in her arms. She held her tight for several minutes, rocking her gently whilst whispering stern words about firework safety. Then she stood up to thank Tom for saving her. Judging by the large patch of foamy dribble on Tom's shoulder, Calypso had already hugged him, so she kissed him on the cheek instead, leaving a pale kiss mark on his smoke-blackened face. Beneath the grime, Tom's face turned red again.

Then dawn broke, and the immediate relief of having put the fire out, and of seeing Slugbucket emerge safe and sound from his new aquatic home, was replaced by concern for more pressing matters. The kitchen table beckoned, so once Tom and Polly had cleaned themselves up, they joined the others in the kitchen for an early morning pot of tea. Polly wrapped her hands around her mug and brought everyone up to date with the night's events. She told them about the voice she'd heard underneath the perch, and about the two people she'd seen running up the drive a few minutes later. That's when Tom suddenly remembered seeing them himself. In all the excitement he'd completely forgotten. Two of them. That's right. And though he'd only caught a brief glimpse, one of them seemed familiar. Then it came to him.

'It was Mr Grub!' he blurted out.

The Captain looked at him, then nodded sadly,

as though somehow that made sense.

'But surely that's impossible,' said Tom. 'Why would a bank manager be creeping around in the middle of the night setting fire to sheds?'

'I have a horrible feeling the answer lies somewhere in our loan contract, Tom,' the Captain replied, almost apologetically. 'But we don't have time to worry about that now. Hundreds of people are due to arrive here tonight expecting to see a fantastic firework display – and there isn't going to be one. We have to decide what to do.'

One by one, the options were put forward.

No, they didn't have either the time or the money to replace the fireworks.

Yes, it was much too late to cancel the event.

Yes, they could invite everyone in for a free glass of Fizzle and a slice of carrot cake, but –

No, it would hardly compensate them for a wasted evening, and –

No, it certainly wouldn't be enough to entice them to join the club – which was, after all, the whole point of having the firework display in the first place.

'We don't have any choice,' the Captain said finally. 'Unless we can think of a proper way to entertain these people and give them a night to remember, we'll have to turn them away at the gates.'

They all had ideas, of course, but nothing that could match the Grand Firework Spectacular that the people of Shipley had been promised and would be expecting. One by one they shook their weary heads. Except for Seymour. He was staring up at the ceiling, which he did whenever he was deep in thought. The Captain leaned across the table towards him.

'Shipmate, do you have any brilliant ideas up those pyjama sleeves of yours?'

'Well,' said Seymour, returning to earth, 'there might be *something* we can do.'

A Change of Plan

'I've been working on it for about a year,' Seymour explained. They were all in the Crow's Nest, standing in a semicircle around Seymour, who was enjoying being the centre of attention.

'A long time ago I noticed – like we all did – that Fizzle wasn't like normal water at all. I'm not talking about the magic,' he assured Tom. 'No, I mean that it behaves differently to other water. You already know that it doesn't lose its fizz, but have you noticed that it goes round the plughole the opposite way to ordinary water?'

A semicircle of shaking heads answered his question.

'Well, it does. Anyway, I started conducting experiments on it and I made a few discoveries.'

Seymour dripped a large droplet of Fizzle on to a glass dish. 'Watch carefully,' he said. Then he reached over to the electric keyboard on the worktop and pressed one of the keys. Tom didn't hear a thing, but the droplet exploded into a hundred smaller droplets, forming the shape of a star.

'Ooooh!' gasped Polly.

Seymour pressed another key and each of the new droplets burst again, forming hundreds of yet smaller stars. 'It works like a dog whistle,' he explained, 'except that I've adapted the keyboard to send out musical notes pitched so high that even dogs can't hear them, only Fizzle can. And when it does, the vibrations of each note make it explode. I can vary the notes, to make differently shaped stars.' He turned to Tom.

'Now, Tom, put your thumb and forefinger together to make a circle.'

Tom did as he was told.

'Now dip it in here and then blow a bubble.' Seymour held up a bucket of soapy-looking Fizzle.

Tom dipped his hand in just far enough to cover the circle, then raised it to his lips and blew. A bubble the size of a grapefruit popped gracefully out of his hand and floated away above his head. Nothing unusual about that, he thought with relief. But then he noticed that the bubble wasn't falling. It was just hanging in the air over him, defying gravity, as if awaiting instructions.

Calypso clapped her hands with delight, before making a grab for Tom's hair.

'Now look at this,' said Seymour. He pressed another note on the keyboard and the bubble burst suddenly. But instead of falling in droplets to the ground, it burst into a hundred smaller bubbles, which continued to float. Seymour played another note and thousands of even smaller bubbles appeared. He continued to press the keys until the bubbles shrank to mist and disappeared. 'There's no end to what this clever stuff can do,' he continued enthusiastically. 'So imagine it on a grand scale, with literally billions of droplets exploding to the sound of music and illuminated with coloured lights. I thought that one day I'd be able to put together a Fizzlework show, spectacular enough to rival any firework display in the world.'

'Well, I'd say that day has come rather sooner than you planned, Seymour,' joked the Captain.

Seymour looked nervous. 'The trouble is that none of it's ready yet. It's all still in my head, and I don't have the equipment I need – hundreds of yards of hosepipe for example, and a water tank and some giant hoops.'

'Anything's possible, shipmate,' insisted the Captain. 'Just tell us what you need and we'll get it for you.'

The room fell silent as Seymour made some mental calculations.

'Well, we'll have to improvise, of course,' he said eventually, 'but we can only try, can't we? Tom, can you and the Captain rustle up a bathtub – come to think of it, one of the sheep's water troughs will do – and carry it up here on to the walkway? Polly, I need two big hoops as well. It doesn't matter what they're made of so long as they're fairly strong and as big as possible – have a look around and see what you can find. Slugbucket, I'm going to need every inch of hosepipe on the estate. You'll have to dismantle the whole garden irrigation system, I'm sorry.'

'Aaar, don't you worry yerself, Seymour,' Slugbucket grinned. 'It'll give me summat to do puttin' it all back agen afterwards.'

'And we're going to need so much power that those treadmills will have to be kept turning all day.'

'I'll go first,' Maggie volunteered. 'Then once Calypso's off to sleep again, I'll be able to help Edna and Constance with the food.'

'Good,' said the Captain. 'Anchors aweigh, then!'

Polly was first on to the walkway and launched herself straight down the slide. Tom and the Captain joined her at the bottom a few seconds later and headed off to find a water trough. Polly made her way to the moat to examine the wheels on Slugbucket's caravan. She had an idea. Sure enough, even though the wheels themselves were burnt beyond use, the metal rims which stretched around their circumference looked undamaged. The caravan had drifted away from the bank slightly, so she hooked it in with her Fizzlestick and hopped aboard. She let the caravan settle in the water before bending down to see if she could remove one of the rims. It would make a perfect hoop. The wood had burnt away from the metal in several places – if she could turn the wheel in the water and loosen the rim all the way round as it came above the surface, it should come off. She fetched Slugbucket's toolkit from inside the caravan, then began turning the wheel and, inch by inch, tapping the metal rim loose with a hammer and chisel. It was then that she noticed something remarkable. Each time she tapped the metal wheel-rim, a Fizzlefish would jump out of the water like a salmon heading upstream. It reminded her of how her leg jumped whenever she crossed her legs and tapped her knee. She would have to tell Seymour about this – maybe they could have dancing Fizzlefish tonight as well? She returned to her task, slowly rotating the wheel in the water until she had tapped most of the metal away from the wood.

Then, with one final knock it slipped off – so easily, in fact, that Polly was sure the Fizzle had helped her. She caught the metal hoop just as it fell into the water and heaved it on board. 'One down, one to go . . .'

By lunchtime, the top of the Crow's Nest looked like the inside of a junk shop, piled high with everything from old taps to bicycle wheels. To Seymour, though, each item was part of a huge and elaborate jigsaw. He'd spent the morning drawing up dozens of little plans and sketches, each showing how something should be constructed, or how it should work, or where it should go. These he now handed to his companions, who set about the afternoon-long task of assembling the equipment in time for the evening's show. Polly's two hoops, for example, were joined together like a pair of giant spectacles and fixed to the outside of the Crow's Nest, so that they could be rotated like the sails of a windmill. As each hoop reached the bottom it would pick up a coating of soapy Fizzle from the water trough which had been positioned below. And as it returned to the top it would be greeted by a jet of air streaming from a large fan placed in one of the Crow's Nest windows. In this way a constant stream of bubbles could be floated out over the house and gardens.

The Crow's Nest sprinkler system was also adapted, so that the four loudspeakers could shoot water straight up into the air, as well as parallel to the ground. Seymour also fitted them with a series of filters, which could be clipped on and off to allow the water to leave the loudspeakers as anything from a solid jet to a fine spray. His mother Constance's old stockings, stretched over the loudspeakers and secured with elastic, like the paper stretched over a jar of home-made jam, produced a particularly fine spray. Lighting was also crucial: a single powerful spotlight was attached to the side of each loudspeaker, enabling a shaft of light to illuminate each jet of water wherever it went. These too had a range of filters, made from small sheets of glass that Maggie had cut to shape and stained with glass paint, and which could be taped over the spotlights at short notice to alter the colour of the beam. Further spotlights, which normally lit up trees in the grounds, were repositioned around the moat and aimed skywards. And whilst Seymour, Tom and Polly were doing all this, Slugbucket and the Captain were laying a single hosepipe around the outside of the moat. Normally it zigzagged up and down between long lines of vegetables in

Slugbucket's garden, evenly soaking the ground via the numerous tiny holes which punctuated its length. But tonight, the holes would direct a thousand fine jets of Fizzle straight up into the air, to create a wall of water around Shipley Manor. All this was time-consuming work, but somehow, by teatime, the main features were in place and the jigsaw had been assembled. Now all it needed was Fizzle to bring it to life.

They gathered one last time in the Crow's Nest to plan the evening's events. The Captain and Seymour had already made a list of the jobs that would need doing, and who should do them, which the Captain read out.

'The Captain – that's me,' he added with a modest grin. 'Master of Ceremonies. My job will be to welcome the visitors and make them feel at home. I'll also be available throughout the evening to show them around, hand out membership applications and make all the announcements. By the way, has anyone seen the brass polish? The buttons on my best uniform are starting to look like mushrooms.'

He peered hopefully over his reading glasses, then continued.

'Seymour: Technical Director. Seymour will be in the Crow's Nest conducting the whole display. He'll be in overall charge, so please watch out for his instructions and follow them as quickly as possible.

'Polly and Tom: Technical Assistants (Crow's Nest). You two will be out on the Crow's Nest walkway aiming the water-jets, changing light filters and churning out those bubbles. I warn you now, you lucky people, that you're going to get very, very wet and messy.'

Polly stole a glance at Tom's reaction. If he was worried about getting a soaking, he certainly wasn't showing it.

'Slugbucket: Technical Assistant (Ground Level). You'll be responsible for the lighting down there, Slugbucket. It's no good having a fantastic display if no one can see it, so your job will be to keep those lights trained on the Fizzle the whole time. Every droplet has to shine out in the darkness.'

'Oh, I'll be good at that,' said Slugbucket. 'I've 'ad lotsa practice searchin' for leaks wi' me torch.'

'Excellent,' said the Captain. 'Now, who's next? Ah yes, Maggie – you're in charge of food and drink.'

'I'm ready to serve,' replied Maggie, pirouetting in her flowery apron. 'I'll take charge of the first-aid box as well,' she added, winking at Polly. 'Just in case we have any snake-bites or other little mishaps.'

Then the Captain's smile widened as he read out the next name.

'Constance,' he announced with a flourish. 'Chief Sheep Impersonator.'

A cheer went up.

'Your chance for stardom has finally arrived, Constance. Seymour will be too busy to talk to the children, so I'd like you to stand in. I'll put some extra feed by the fence, so the sheep should be chewing away there when the children arrive. As soon as they walk past you can talk to them through Seymour's microphone here.' He tapped the top of the microphone with his finger. 'How's your sheep-talk these days?'

'Oh, not b-a-a-a-a-d, thank you, dear, not b-a-a-a-a-d,' replied Constance, winning herself a round of applause.

Finally the Captain turned to Edna.

'Edna: Music. I've twisted Edna's arm, everybody, and she's agreed to bring her saxophone out of retirement, just for tonight.'

A murmur of appreciation went round the room.

'How's it going, Edna?'

Although she looked as frail and nervous as ever,

there was a rock-solid confidence in her reply.

'Well, I've dusted the old thing off and spent a couple of hours practising in the cellar,' she told them. 'Don't worry, we'll have a blast.'

Polly turned to Tom and whispered in his ear.

'Edna used to be one of the best saxophonists in the country. The Captain says she's got lungs like hot water bottles and can blow a note for a whole hour without stopping for breath. Something to do with being able to breathe in and blow out at the same time.'

'Well, if that's all, I think we'd better get going,' said the Captain, clapping his hands together. 'By the way, Seymour –'

Seymour looked up.

'Yes, Captain?'

'I think you can change out of your pyjamas now.'

One by one they left the Crow's Nest to make their final preparations. Saxophones were polished, uniforms pressed, trestle tables laid out with food and drink. Seymour inspected the water-pipes and tightened any loose seals, Slugbucket checked his lights and Polly and Tom stepped inside the treadmills to charge up the generator one last time before the show.

Then, at eight o'clock, the entire population of Shipley appeared from nowhere.

The Fabulous Fizzleworks Show

A tidal wave of expectant children flowed over the gates and down the driveway. Their parents, less adventurous for the most part, streamed in through the little red door. There they were met by the Captain, who greeted each and every one of them, dressed for the occasion in his finest uniform, complete with naval sword. He had timed the show carefully, so that as they descended the driveway the visitors would see Shipley Manor at its most glorious, bathed in the warm amber glow of the setting sun. They would then have time to explore the grounds and treat themselves to a Fizzle Cocktail before darkness fell and the main event got under way.

Shortly after eight o'clock, an extremely smart,

kind-looking man with razor-sharp creases down the front of his jeans approached the Captain with a friendly smile.

'How do you do?' he said. 'I'm Roger Sterling, Tom's father. You must be the Captain.'

'Indeed I am,' said the Captain, gripping Roger's hand and shaking it vigorously. 'I'm very pleased to meet you. And may I congratulate you on your son. He's become a very important member of our crew here, you know.'

Roger blushed, almost lost for words. 'Oh well, I'm glad . . .'

'So important, in fact,' continued the Captain, 'that you won't be seeing him at all until after the show. We've got him up in the rigging tonight, performing some very important duties. But as soon as the show's over, I promise to send him down to you. Now tell me,' asked the Captain, leaning closer, 'is your Mr Grub going to be joining us later?'

Oddly enough, Roger had been into Grub's office earlier that day to ask the same question. Grub's reply had puzzled him. He had closed his file and slumped back in his chair, a thin smile stretched wide across his face. Then he had looked Roger up and down rather dismissively, and answered in a slow, can't-be-bothered voice.

'Oh, I think I'll give it a miss, Sterling – something tells me it won't be up to much.'

What he'd meant by that, Roger couldn't imagine. After all, Mr Grub knew full well that Shipley Manor had spent a small fortune on fireworks.

'Well, I've been telling him all about it,' said Roger. 'In fact, he's always very interested in anything to do with Tom and Shipley Manor, but he says he's unable to come tonight.' That wasn't exactly what he'd said, of course, but Roger thought it sounded less insulting.

'Perhaps he doesn't think it will be up to much,' said the Captain.

Roger was taken aback. How had the Captain guessed that?

'I've no idea why he would think that,' he said, honestly. Because, of course, he hadn't.

The Captain's face softened into a sympathetic, understanding smile.

'Of course not,' he said. 'Now if you'll excuse me, Mr Sterling – Roger – I really should welcome a few more people. Please enjoy the show – Tom's put a lot of hard work into it.'

Roger departed to explore the gardens, and as dusk gave way to darkness, the stream of people became a trickle. Once the reporter from the *Shipley Gazette* had bustled through the doorway with his photographer in tow, the Captain pulled out his pocket watch and decided that it was show time. Briskly, he made his way up to the triangular balcony which overlooked the gardens at the front of the house. Edna was already there, unpacking her saxophone. Below and behind him he could see Seymour and Slugbucket. They both signalled to him that they were ready. Edna slipped the saxophone strap around her delicate neck and gave him a short nod. The Captain took a deep breath.

'Shipmates,' he boomed. A thousand heads swivelled up to look at him. 'Welcome to Shipley Manor. Owing to circumstances beyond our control we are unable to present the firework display which we had planned for this evening.' A murmur of surprise and disappointment rippled through the audience. 'However,' he boomed twice as loudly, 'we have prepared a spectacular alternative. Ladies and gentlemen, for the first time ever, anywhere in the world, may I present – FIZZLEWORKS!'

In the hush and darkness that followed, a lone, continuous note sailed up into the air over the audience's heads. Suddenly a single spotlight flashed on, illuminating Edna on the balcony, standing like a figurehead at the bow of a ship. With the saxophone to her lips, and her eyes tight shut, she held the note for so long that some feared she might pass out. But she had only just begun. She was imagining water: trickling, flowing, meander-ing, cascading, whirling, crashing. This would be her inspiration. Then she really began to play. At first the long, slow notes drifted down the valley like a warm mist, enveloping the audience. Gradually, the sound grew louder and more intense, as if a thunderstorm was building and gathering pace towards them. Finally, it arrived, and taking his cue from the music, Seymour launched four jets of Fizzle into the night sky. As the first drops reached their summit and started to fall back to earth, Edna leaned back and puffed out her cheeks. As she filled the valley with yet more sound, Slugbucket fired every light up into the sky and Seymour pressed the first note on the keyboard. The top of each jet exploded into an enormous shimmering star, and the audience roared its approval. Seymour pressed again and again, and the cascades sparkled and scattered into ever smaller stars as they fell towards the ground in a fine, refreshing mist. Luminous jets of Fizzle continued to shoot skywards, sending layer upon layer of glistening, brightly coloured stars up into the night like liquid ash from an erupting volcano. As children ran about trying to catch the falling stars in their hands, Seymour moved frantically around the circular worktop in the Crow's Nest, watching the action unfold outside, adjusting water pressure, playing the highly tuned keyboard in time with Edna's music, and shouting instructions to

Tom and Polly. He was the maestro conducting his orchestra, and he was determined to give the performance of his life.

'Divert all water north.'

'Fit fine spray filters – now!'

'Aim water straight up.'

'Orange light filters. Come on, quickly, before the next starburst.'

Polly and Tom ran around the walkway, desperately trying to keep up with the action and with no time to look up and admire the show. As Edna reached the climax of her piece, Seymour instructed them to aim the jets so that they met at a single point high up above the Crow's Nest. Then he pressed different keys in rapid succession, so that a single massive star seemed to be changing shape continuously as it fell towards the roof. As the water hit the Crow's Nest he pressed again, and the star exploded, as if shattered against the building. Edna unleashed a torrent of tumbling, crashing notes as the water hit the building. And then the first piece of music was over.

Polly and Tom were soaked to the skin. But they didn't have time to worry about that, or to listen to the deafening applause that had broken out in the grounds. Seymour was signalling for them to prepare the bubble machine. At Seymour's command they started to rotate the heavy hoops through the soapy Fizzle and up past the window. Then the fan did its work, sending bubbles the size of elephants floating gracefully out over the garden. There they gathered, bobbing above people's heads like a shimmering glass ceiling, blotting out the sky and reflecting the awestruck faces of the people below. Again Edna started quietly, slowly building up the volume and tempo to a huge crescendo: Seymour's cue to burst the bubbles. When he did, the entire audience ducked, expecting to get a soaking. But instead, the bubbles continued to float, multiplying and growing like a giant flower bursting into bloom. The moment the bubbles reached the point beyond which they could multiply no further, they disappeared in a puff of mist. But as soon as they had gone, Polly and Tom sent out another long line of bubbles from the Crow's Nest. This time Seymour burst them as they travelled along, creating lines of foam in the sky like coloured jet trails. Adjusting the fan, Polly and Tom then sent out bubbles in different formations, looping and spiralling and zigzagging their way across the sky, filling it with abstract coloured shapes just like an enormous painting. Finally they sent a single row of bubbles out in a graceful arc over the grounds and, signalling to Slugbucket to turn on every light at once, watched as the arc turned suddenly into a glorious, glittering rainbow. The audience gasped in appreciation, but there was even more to come.

As Edna began her last tune, Seymour directed the water up through the sprinkler system which the Captain and Slugbucket had stretched around the moat. A shimmering wall of silver water rose into the air around Shipley Manor, encircling it like a huge cinema screen. And now it was time for the main performance. This time Seymour played the keyboard as it should be played. Matching Edna note for note, he ran his fingers up and down the keys like a concert pianist, transforming the screen into a dazzling spectacle of moving images, like some vast liquid kaleidoscope. The screen played host to an endless variety of shapes and colours, each flashing in front of the audience for no more than a split second before giving way to the next startling image. As the show edged closer and closer to its climax, Seymour sent fine sprays down from the top of the Crow's Nest to meet the wall of water below, so that Shipley Manor was encased in a single dome of shimmering Fizzle. Then he stopped playing. As it settled, the dome of water turned smooth and reflective until, like the perfect camouflage, it became a seamless continuation of the woods and sky which surrounded it. The effect, better than

Seymour could possibly have hoped for, was to render Shipley Manor invisible.

And now it was down to Edna to bring the show to its finale. Her eyes tight shut, she pictured being carried along a raging torrent towards a waterfall of unimaginable height. She played furiously as the water crashed and ricocheted against the rocks in a white-water frenzy. And then she was over the edge. A long, continuous note signalled her fall and carried her down, deeper and deeper into the abyss. Still she blew. Then far below, the bottom of the waterfall appeared, beckoning her into its foaming jaws. At the very moment she hit the water she raised her arm and Seymour pressed the last note of the evening. A billion droplets exploded simultaneously and in an instant Shipley Manor reappeared as if from nowhere, illuminated against the night sky.

'Magic,' gasped Polly.

Then all was quiet, except for the faint hiss of Fizzle as it made its way discreetly back into the earth.

Finally, a lone voice cracked the stunned silence. 'Bravo!' cried Mr Tutt, 'bravo-o-o' – and set off an avalanche of applause which engulfed Shipley Manor. Seymour emerged from the Crow's Nest and punched the air in triumph. Polly and Tom joined him to take a bow, and Edna, her saxophone still slung around her neck, stepped back modestly into the spotlight to acknowledge the appreciation of the crowd. Down below, Slugbucket and the Captain hooked arms and performed a celebratory jig.

Then the bonfire was lit and the party really began, the air abuzz with talk of the display, and how the water had behaved as if it were almost . . . magical. Maggie – assisted by Constance, who had finished her sheep-impersonating duties for the night – was soon swamped with demand for Fizzle Cocktails and food. As the two women served their hungry and thirsty customers, Seymour set up another stall selling jam-jars filled with soapy Fizzle and hoops made from old coat-hangers. He couldn't sell them fast enough: it seemed that everybody wanted a chance to make their own mini-Fizzlework display. Beside him, the Captain handed out membership forms to a long line of potential Shipley Manor Country Club members. First in the queue were Mr Tutt and his wife, who joined the club there and then, handing over a cheque for their yearly subscription. The Captain waved the money towards Maggie next door as if to say, 'See, everything's going to be all right.' But what with holding Calypso in one arm and serving up a plateful of Caribbean coconut fritters with the other, she was far too busy to notice.

Polly and Tom came down from the Crow's Nest

and went in search of Tom's father. They spotted him down by the bonfire. He was sipping a Fizzle Cocktail, which he raised cheerfully to show that he'd seen them. But as they approached him Tom could see his expression changing, and it suddenly occurred to him why. Though Tom had made an effort to clean himself up earlier in the day, it had been a rather rushed and half-hearted affair. Now, much of the remaining dirt and smoke from the previous night's fire had run out of his hair and down his face in long Fizzle-soaked streaks. He was wet and filthy from head to foot, and despite feeling happier than he'd ever felt in his life, he didn't look well. Dark grey bags from lack of sleep lay heavily under his eyes, and Roger could see the numerous minor cuts and bruises which Tom had accumulated the night before. Worst of all, he smelled of . . . burning. On closer examination Roger saw that not only were Tom's clothes totally ruined, his hair had been scorched and his eyebrows almost burned to a crisp.

Then Roger's gaze moved to Polly, who was still dressed as a firework, albeit one which had recently gone off. Her condition was even more disturbing, given that she was that much younger, and hadn't made nearly as much effort as Tom to clean herself up. Roger's mouth pinched tight in a look of distaste, and Tom could see that an explanation was urgently required. So he told him about sleeping in the woods, about the explosion in the shed and the fire which followed. Finally, he told him about how he thought he'd seen Mr Grub running up the driveway. Roger listened in stony silence, his face set somewhere between anger and disgust as the story unfolded. What kind of place was this, letting children sleep out in the woods unsupervised and without so much as a tent? And as for the fireworks, how could the people here have exposed Tom to such dangers? He could have been killed. It was reckless irresponsibility, pure and simple. And now here was Tom trying to lay the blame on Mr Grub, the manager of Shipley Bank for goodness sake. His boss.

Roger Sterling's world shifted under his feet. He wanted order, responsibility and duty to prevail in the world, and evidently there wasn't much of that to be had at Shipley Manor. Much as he had liked the Captain and been flattered by his praise for Tom, he didn't want his son exposed to the eccentricities of such people, whose obvious disregard for normal standards of conduct didn't conform to his idea of 'the right way to do things' at all. Rules were important. People who broke them were a menace to themselves and everyone else. What were they teaching Tom here? Sleeping rough, playing with fireworks, walking around like a scarecrow. What next – playing truant from school?

His thoughts were interrupted by a flash bulb bursting over his shoulder as the *Shipley Gazette* photographer took a picture of Polly and Tom.

'Do you mind!' he complained, uncharacteristically. He looked around him. Shipley Manor had suddenly lost all its charm.

'I think we should go,' he said stiffly, and Tom knew better than to argue.

Read All About It

Not a word was said on the way home. Tom stared straight ahead through the car windscreen, devastated that his wonderful evening had ended so sourly. When they got back he thanked his father for the lift home and went immediately upstairs. He knew what he had to do. He emerged an hour later, spotlessly clean and smelling of soap, hair combed and wearing his pyjamas, dressing gown and slippers. Normality. He knew his father would still be angry with him and he would rather have stayed in his room. Nevertheless, he had promised the Captain that he would do something. He went into the kitchen where his father was making cocoa and slipped the Shipley Manor loan contract quietly on to the table. His father turned round.

'What's that, Tom?' he asked.

'It's to do with the loan that the Captain took out with Shipley Bank,' replied Tom. 'The Captain thinks it could explain why Mr Grub was in the grounds the other night. I said you might be willing to take a look at it.'

Roger bowed his head in desperation. That bunch of eccentrics at Shipley Manor had obviously filled Tom's head with complete nonsense. He took two mugs of cocoa to the table and sat down opposite his son.

'Now look, Tom,' he said patiently. 'Shipley Bank has been in existence for over two hundred years. It's one of the town's oldest and most respected institutions, and Mr Grub is its manager. He's not some common thief – he doesn't run around breaking into people's property and setting their sheds on fire. He's a bank manager. He belongs to the golf club, for heaven's sake!'

'But I *saw* him!' Tom pleaded.

'You can't have done, Tom,' Roger insisted forcefully, his head shaking in denial, his lips pursed tightly together as if to hold in his certainty. 'It's *absolutely impossible*.'

Later that night, Tom lay in bed staring up at the ceiling. He couldn't sleep. He realised that for the past few months he'd been living in two different worlds and now he didn't know where he was any more. He wanted to know what to believe in, *who* to believe in. Perhaps his father was right. Perhaps the people at Shipley Manor were irresponsible. At the very least they'd managed to confuse him, so that he didn't know what was expected of him any more, or how to behave. He'd even started to think there might be something magical about that Fizzle after all. Not that he would admit that to anyone – it was hardly grown up, was it? Perhaps his father was right about that too. Perhaps Shipley Manor had simply filled his head with silly, childish ideas and turned him into a dreamer like Polly. He rolled over on to his side. But he'd been having so much *fun* there, and Polly and her family had become his friends. And what if his father was wrong? What if Mr Grub *had* been there that night? That would turn everything upside down, wouldn't it? He had to know. He closed his eyes and replayed the events of the previous night in the hope of seeing them more clearly. He was back there now, standing on the perch, looking out into the darkness. Where was Polly? His eyes followed the track down to the house, then up along the driveway towards the trees. And there they were again: two figures running off into the distance. He screwed his eyes tighter and strained to get a closer look, a sharper focus. He could see them more clearly now. The spindly woman running in front he'd never seen before. But the man puffing away behind her – that was a different matter. Tom definitely recognised him. It was Mr Grub.

Venetia Pike sat at her dressing table stroking Viceroy, her boa constrictor, which she had draped like a scarf around her shoulders.

She and Grub had watched the final, blazing destruction of Shipley Manor's fireworks from the safety of a nearby hill. So she knew that the Captain's plans to relaunch Shipley Manor Country Club had literally gone up in smoke, along with any chance he may have had of repaying the massive debt he owed to Shipley Bank.

Tomorrow it would be two weeks exactly since Mr Tutt's second inspection, the date when, according to the loan contract, the entire sum of money was due to be paid back. The Captain still didn't know that, of course, and even now he would be going through his trouser pockets hoping to scrape up enough cash for a small monthly repayment. But when Grub arrived he wouldn't be interested in that. Oh no. When Pike's pungent partner wafted up to the main door of Shipley Manor, he would be there to demand the whole lot.

The Captain would assume, at first, that the bank manager had made a simple mistake. But then Grub would point to the small print in the loan contract – his Killer Clause – stating that if the Captain didn't repay the loan in full, straight away, the bank would become the new owners of Shipley Manor. The Captain wouldn't be able to, of course, so he would beg for more time to find the money. 'Certainly,' Grub would agree, raising the Captain's hopes momentarily. 'I'll give you one hour.'

And then it would be up to Venetia. With her voice disguised through the folds of a silk scarf, Pike would telephone the Captain and offer to buy Shipley Manor on behalf of the Shipley Property Investment Company. She wouldn't offer much for it, of course, but once the Captain had repaid the bank loan he would, at least, be able to feed his children for a few months and put a roof over their heads. And so he would accept. She smiled at her own ruthlessness. 'In businessss you have to crush the life out of your opponent,' she mused. 'Isn't that right, Viceroy?'

Suddenly she felt a burning desire to call Mr Tutt, whom she knew had planned to go to the Shipley Manor Firework Spectacular. The event had been ruined, that much was certain. But still she hankered after the gory details of how Shipley's townsfolk had arrived expecting a fabulous night's entertainment, only to be greeted by the Captain's grovelling apologies. And how, besieged by hordes of angry parents and crying children, he had finally sunk to his knees, broken, humiliated and penniless. Although she knew it would all be reported in the following morning's *Shipley Gazette*, Pike simply couldn't wait that long. So she called Mr Tutt. Stroking Viceroy gently, she settled back in her chair and prepared to luxuriate in Mr Tutt's account of the disastrous evening as if it were a long, hot, relaxing bath.

Instead, what she got was an ice-cold shower.

By the time Mr Tutt had concluded his detailed and (as always) thorough account of Shipley Manor's triumphant Fizzlework display, Pike's bony knuckles had turned white round Viceroy's neck and the pressure of her grip had caused his eyes to bulge half-way out of their sockets. He looked surprised. After all, wasn't he the one supposed to do the squeezing around here?

As soon as Mr Tutt had finished talking, Pike thanked him politely through gritted teeth and replaced the phone. Then she stared at it with wild eyes for a few seconds, before hurling it like a slingshot across the room. It shattered on impact. She looked down at Viceroy. 'Sorry about that, ssssweetie,' she said. 'Mummy's got a little problem she needs to ssssort out.' She dropped him back into his terrarium and reached for her wig. A short while later the whole house shook as she slammed the front door behind her. It was time to finish this once and for all.

She entered the Council building, all malevolence and clicking heels, and swept up to the top floor. Without removing her jacket, she went straight to her desk and pulled out a cassette. She pushed it into the tape recorder, sat back in her chair and stabbed the 'Play' button with her fingernail.

It was Polly's voice.

'Oh, I've never been to school . . .' she was saying.

Pike wound the tape on a little further.

' . . . and then we get the children to work in the kitchens . . . Oh no, we don't pay them . . .'

Perfect, she thought – it always pays to carry a little tape recorder around with you. A spot of creative editing and the *Shipley Gazette* will have the scoop of the year.

Pike prodded the 'Stop' button and called the editor of the *Shipley Gazette*.

'Charles,' she purred. 'Venetia Pike here. I understand you're running a story about Shipley Manor in tomorrow's *Gazette*.'

'That's right, Venetia. We're writing a piece for the leisure section on page nine. "Fizzlework Fantasia" is the headline: "Local country club set to become Shipley's most popular visitor attraction after –"'

Pike interrupted him.

'Forget page nine, Charles. I've got a story about Shipley Manor that's going to blow your socks off.'

'Well, we're going to press in a few minutes, Venetia . . .'

'Believe me, Charles, it's the biggest scandal ever to hit Shipley.'

'Even so, I'm not sure we have time to –'

Then Pike played her trump card.

'By the way, Charles, have we granted planning permission for your attic conversion yet?' There was a pause.

'I'll hold the front page,' he said eventually.

Pike allowed herself the luxury of a smile.

By the time I've finished with Shipley Manor, she thought, it will be about as popular as a python in a playpen.

Tom woke up early on Monday morning. He'd spent most of Sunday catching up on his sleep and avoiding contact with his father, who he knew was on the verge of forbidding him to return to Shipley Manor. If only he could get himself ready and out of the house without the subject arising, then perhaps he could go there straight from school as if nothing had happened. He put on his school uniform and went downstairs. As he walked into the kitchen he could see that something was wrong.

Though his father must have heard him come in, he didn't acknowledge him. Instead he seemed transfixed by the copy of the *Shipley Gazette* which lay on the table in front of him. Tom peered over his shoulder. Staring up at him from the front page of the *Gazette* was the startled face of a ragged young girl. Thick with grime, wearing torn and burned clothing, there was no mistaking who it was. Polly. The headline underneath screamed in his face: CHILD SLAVERY MASQUERADING AS HOLIDAY CAMP. Tom felt sick. He craned his neck forward and read the article.

This newspaper has learned that Shipley Manor, the well-known local country club owned by Captain Horatio Shipley, has for many years been using deprived inner-city children as unpaid labour in its gardens and kitchens. Documentary evidence, obtained from reliable sources in the Council, confirms a catalogue of abuse and exploitation, culminating recently in the near-death of this child in an explosion of unlicensed fireworks. It has also come to the newspaper's attention that children residing at Shipley Manor have been withheld from school, and are often left to fend for themselves at night, in the surrounding snake-infested woods. Venetia Pike, Chief Executive of Shipley Council, has assured this newspaper that, because of the child safety issues at stake, action will be taken immediately.

Tom's father looked round at him. 'That's it, Tom. I'm not having you set foot in that place again.'

The tension that had been welling up inside Tom suddenly exploded.

'But it's all lies, Dad, every word of it.'

His father stood up, waving the newspaper at him.

'Of course it's not lies. It's right here in black and white on the front page of the *Shipley Gazette* – what more proof do you need? Be realistic, Tom: how can I possibly let you near the place after reading this? Last night was bad enough, but this . . .'

He dropped the newspaper back on to the table.

'But it's all lies, Dad,' repeated Tom.

'So you mean this little girl *does* go to school then, does she?' said his father.

'Well, no,' said Tom. 'Or rather, yes, but –'

'So she doesn't,' said his father. 'And another thing: you've been working there for months now, and not once have I seen you come home with any wages. I bet they haven't paid you a single penny, have they?'

Tom was cut short. His father was right. But he knew it was only because the Captain had had so much else to think about. He knew he'd be paid some time.

'Well, no, but –'

'But nothing, Tom. I wasn't sure what to think

about the place after Saturday, I admit, but this –'
he said, slapping the front of the newspaper with
the back of his hand. 'Well, Tom, you can forget it.
I have a duty to protect you. In fact, if you must
know, I'm disgusted with myself for letting you
work there without checking the place out first.'

By now Tom was choking back tears.

'But they're not like that, Dad, they're really nice
people. It must be something to do with Mr Grub.'

'Don't you *dare* mention Mr Grub to me again,
Tom. I'm taking this into the office right now to
show him. The bank has lent Shipley Manor a
great deal of money – on my recommendation, I
might add – and he'll need to know about this as
soon as possible.'

'The Captain believes me,' Tom shouted. 'Why
can't you be more like him?'

His father winced, then glared angrily at his son.

'Captain Shipley is a rule-breaker, Tom,' he
reminded him. 'Just like the man who killed your
mother. Now get yourself to school and we'll talk
about it tonight.'

Then he stuffed the newspaper into his briefcase
and left for work.

At the same time, in the offices of Shipley Council,
Pike had been busy assembling her forces like a

general preparing for a final, crushing victory. The powers under her command were awesome: the newspaper, public opinion, the bank, the full authority and resources of the Council – and now, finally, the police.

'Yes, Chief Constable, I'm sure you've seen the front page of the *Gazette*. The Council's switchboard has been overwhelmed with calls from concerned members of the public. We've assured them that children's welfare is indeed our highest priority and that we shall be closing Shipley Manor down immediately. I've instructed all the relevant Council departments to converge on Shipley Manor at noon. I understand also that a representative from Shipley Bank will be there with his bailiffs to recover a substantial unpaid loan. Yes, the usual police presence would be very welcome. Thank you for your support, Chief Constable.'

She put the phone down but kept hold of it, drumming the top with her fingernail.

Right then, she thought, I suppose I'd better call my odious little friend and tell him what's going on.

As soon as he arrived at the bank, Roger straightened his tie and knocked on Barclay Grub's door. There was no reply. He was probably in the middle of a phone call. Normally, Roger would have gone away and come back later. But this was important. He decided to nip in quietly and leave the newspaper on his boss's desk. Grub's eyes flicked up coldly as he walked in.

'Yes, I'll call the bailiffs on the way and get them to meet us there. Now I must go, someone's wandered into my office uninvited.' He put the phone down impatiently. 'What is it, Sterling? Can't you see I'm busy?'

'I'm sorry, Mr Grub, but I thought you ought to see this as soon as possible.' Roger held the newspaper out to him, but Grub waved it away.

'I already know about that,' he said dismissively. 'I didn't get where I am today without being at least three steps ahead of the rest of you. For your information, Sterling, I've just been informed that the Council is planning to close Shipley Manor down immediately. It looks like they're well and truly finished, so unless Captain Shipley can pay the bank back in full straight away, he's going to lose his property. That should wipe the smile off the old seadog's face – assuming the Council's Child Protection Team haven't done it first, of course. Now, if you'll excuse me, some of us have work to do.'

He grabbed his case and headed for the door.

'You know, Sterling,' he said, turning to Roger from the doorway, 'I'm really quite surprised that you allowed your son to work at a place like that – grossly irresponsible, if you ask me. Don't forget to close the door on your way out.'

Roger stared numbly at the empty doorway. For the past few months Grub had been fairly pleasant to him, friendly even, and always interested in what Tom was doing. But today . . . He turned back to the desk. What should he do with the *Gazette*? He decided he should leave it there for Grub anyway, so he dropped it on the desk alongside a file marked 'Shipley Property Investments'. The name caught his eye, not least because it was a company he'd never heard of before. It certainly wasn't one of the bank's clients. The bottom of a letter protruded from the file, with three words clearly visible: 'Director: Barclay Grub'. Something inside Roger urged him to take a closer look. Tom's suspicions and Grub's rude outburst had suddenly combined to open a wafer-thin crack in Roger's rock-solid respect for his boss's authority. And the way he seemed to welcome the bad news about Shipley Manor – well, that was most odd. He glanced round to check that he was alone, then opened the file. Inside, he found a list of properties. They had all once belonged to customers of Shipley Bank, but now, according to this list, they were owned by the Shipley Property Investment Company – directors: Venetia Pike and

Barclay Grub. He looked down the list. Each business had gone bust owing the bank money, usually as a result of a dispute with Shipley Council or some unexplained accident. And each time their property had been bought by the Shipley Property Investment Company for a fraction of its real value, then redeveloped or sold on at a huge profit. Factories, farm buildings, restaurants. At the bottom of the list, in brackets, was the name of what Roger now realised to be the company's latest victim: Shipley Manor.

Everything started to fall into place. Grub's interest in Shipley Manor, his eagerness to lend them money and now his barely concealed glee at the prospect of their downfall. Tom had been right after all. Grub was nothing more than a cheap crook. Suddenly Roger felt empty. Where once there had been loyalty to his boss and respect for his authority, there was now nothing but a hollow, sickening void. He slumped back on the edge of Grub's desk. If you couldn't trust a bank manager, who could you trust? The answer soon came to him. Tom, of course, that's who. Tom had been trying to tell him about Grub all along. And what had he done? Ignored him, his own son, simply because he couldn't bear to think that his boss might be a crook. How could he have been so blind? He had to speak to Tom. He had to tell him he was sorry, and that he believed him, and that somehow he would try to make things right. He picked up the phone and called Tom's school. He wasn't there. There was only one place he could have gone instead. Roger scooped up the file and the newspaper and rushed out of Grub's office, leaving the door wide open behind him.

When Grub was half-way down the road, en route to his rendezvous with Pike, an alarm bell rang inside his head. He screeched to a halt and reached over to his briefcase. The file wasn't inside. He thought back. He'd been about to put it in his briefcase when Sterling had walked in. He must have left it there on his desk, right in front of him. He turned his car round and sped back towards the bank. It would be all right. Sterling didn't have any reason to go nosing around on his desk – and even if he did, he wouldn't have the guts. As he tore into the car park he saw Roger leaving through the exit on the other side. Even at a distance he could see the expression on his face. Grim. Determined. It didn't look good. He threw open the car door and ran back into his office. Sure enough, the file had gone. How could he have been so careless? Like a fool, the smell of victory had distracted him, and now he was paying the price. But there was still time. He and Venetia could still be Lord and Lady of the Manor. He would catch Sterling and retrieve that file, no matter what the cost. Now, where would he be going with it? Shipley Manor. It had to be. He'd be on his way there now to warn them. He ran back to the car park. Even allowing for Sterling's head start, his sports car would get him there first.

Slugbucket's Pit

But Roger didn't go straight to Shipley Manor. First he drove home to examine the Shipley Manor loan contract, which had remained unopened on the kitchen table. He flicked directly to the back and started to read the hundreds of lines of small print, rapidly moving his head from side to side like a spectator at a tennis match. When he found what he was looking for, he threw the document into his briefcase and leaped back into his car.

He slid to a gravelly halt outside Shipley Manor and ran through the little red door into the grounds. As soon as he stepped on to the driveway, a heavy branch struck him across his back, sending him tumbling down the steep bank into the woods. He came to rest face down among the decaying roots of a storm-ravaged tree-trunk, into which was carved the leering, predatory face of Mad Jack Flint, reputedly the bloodthirstiest pirate ever to sail the high seas. Slowly, feeling as though his whole body had turned to lead, Roger raised himself on to all fours and crawled towards his briefcase, which had fallen just out of arm's reach. But before he could get to it, another blow came crashing down, this time across the back of his head. The ground rose up to meet him, filling his mouth with dirt.

'Do you really think I'm prepared to live on the pittance the bank pays me for looking after idiots like you?' sneered Grub. 'It's nothing but pocket money.'

His puffy, wheezing voice was unmistakable, as was the sickly smell of sweat and after-shave which accompanied it. But Roger had to see him with his own eyes. Even though every movement sent pain screaming through his body, he forced himself up on to one elbow and rolled over on to his back. Barclay Grub stood over him, black against a dazzling halo of morning sun.

'You haven't had a clue what's been going on, have you, Sterling?' he spat contemptuously. 'You've ambled into my office day after day, week after week, wittering on about Tom and his precious job here at Shipley Manor. Did you really think that I was interested in you or that son of yours? All I wanted to know about was this place. You and Tom were my spies, my very own undercover agents. And you know what happens to spies when they get caught, don't you?'

Roger curled himself up into a tight protective ball, as Grub raised the thick branch above his head once more. But as his boss arched backwards ready to strike, a sliver of sun cleared the top of his head. The narrow gash of light flashed across Mad Jack's face, instantly drawing Grub's attention to it. He looked up, and as he did so Mad Jack's eyes seemed to flare into life and stare directly at him. Grub cried out and lurched backwards, stumbling over a fallen branch and landing with a heavy flop on his back. He was expecting to be hurt, but he wasn't. In fact, as he lay there spread-eagled, he could feel that the ground beneath him was actually quite soft. And it was moving. Fear and revulsion washed over him as he realised that he had landed in the middle of the gardener's slug pit, which Roger had once told him about. And he was about to be engulfed, for the impact of his body hitting the surface had caused a huge ripple – a metre-high wave of slugs – which was now moving away from him towards the edge of the pit. In a matter of seconds it would rebound against the side and roll back towards him. He knew he had to get out of there fast, but the more he tried to move the further he sank. All he could do was lie flat and perfectly still, feeling the slugs making their way up his sleeves and trouser legs and down his collar. He could feel them on his skin, wrapping themselves around his fingers, moving over his face, exploring the insides of his ears. He closed his mouth tight shut and tried to breathe through his nose. At the same time he turned his head, and from the corner of his eye he saw that the wave had reached the edge of the pit and was on its way back towards him. There was nothing he could do. By now two slugs had slipped silently into his nose so that he could no longer breathe through it. He screwed his eyes tight shut and tried to hold his breath for as long as possible until finally, when his burning lungs felt as though they were about to explode, he opened his mouth wide to take one last gulp of air. But it was not air that filled his lungs. At that moment the approaching wave crashed down over him, filling his mouth with his new sluggy friends and pushing him deep into the slimy darkness of Slugbucket's pit.

When Grub's blow didn't come, Roger uncurled himself and looked around. Grub had disappeared. Stranger still, Roger's briefcase, containing proof of his boss's trickery, lay unopened where he'd dropped it. Surely that was what Grub had been after – so why hadn't he taken it? Still in such pain that he was barely able to move, he dug his fingers into the earth and clawed his way over to his briefcase. He checked the contents – everything was still there. Now, if only he could make it down to the house. He grasped the handle and tried to get to his feet. Half-way up, everything went black.

When he awoke, his first thought was that he'd been in a fire. He was hanging upside down, slung fireman-style over a strong pair of shoulders, his nostrils clogged with the smell of wood smoke. But the shoulders belonged to Slugbucket, and the burning smell came from Slugbucket's old gardening jacket, which had been smoked like a kipper on the night of the fire (along with everything else in his caravan) and which was now brushing up against Roger's face. Roger's head felt as though it was filled with concrete. Even so, with a huge effort he managed to raise it just enough to recognise Polly marching along behind him, carrying her Fizzlestick in one hand and his briefcase in the other.

'Hello, Mr Sterling. This is Slugbucket,' she said. 'We found you in the woods.'

Then he remembered what had happened. He tried to speak: 'Mizza Grub . . . hit me wizza stick . . .'

'Don't you try ter speak, Mister Sterlin',' said Slugbucket, striding on down the Beastlybark Trail. 'Let's jus' worry 'bout gettin' you inside so Maggie can take a good look at yer. Not far ter go now.'

The Captain met them as they emerged from the woods and Tom, looking anxious and frightened, rushed out to meet them on the drawbridge. He'd never seen his father hurt and helpless like this before – he was normally so fit and strong.

'I'm sorry, Dad,' he said. 'I just *had* to warn the Captain about the newspaper story and to tell him I knew it was all lies. I was going to go to school afterwards, really I was.'

'No . . . *I'm* sorry, Tom,' said Roger breathlessly, his voice still slurred. 'You were right . . . 'bout Mizza Grub . . . sorry I din' believe you . . . An' my apol'gies to you, Cap'n Shipley . . . fer gettin' you . . . involved wiv 'im . . .' He gestured weakly towards Polly. 'You need to . . . look in my briefcase . . . page eight, clause . . . nine, subsection three . . .'

'Well, let's sort you out first, shall we, shipmate?' said the Captain. 'Check you haven't got any broken bones. Tom, would you run ahead and hold the kitchen door open for us, please?'

They took Roger into the kitchen and laid him flat on the table, then Slugbucket headed back outside to make sure their unwanted visitor wasn't still lurking around. Maggie appeared a few seconds later carrying the first-aid box.

'I've left Calypso with Constance,' she informed the Captain quietly. Then, turning to Roger, she said, 'Now let's sort you out, shall we, Mr Sterling?'

'Right,' said the Captain, 'I think we should let Maggie get on with her work. Tom, I'm sure you'd like to stay with your father. The rest of us will wait in the cocktail lounge. Call us on the blowpipe if you need us, Maggie.'

Edna and Seymour were already waiting for them in the lounge. Nautipus was on Seymour's lap, gazing hungrily through one of the portholes at a Siamese fighting fish that seemed to be circling endlessly in the water outside, as if trying to bite its own tail. Polly will have to hook that one out and oil its hinges, Seymour thought. The table in front of them was littered with empty Fizzle bottles, the remains of a very happy hour spent the previous evening counting the takings from the Fizzlework display. They had done well. The money raised from the food and drink stall and from new membership subscriptions had far exceeded their expectations, and filled the three glass jars which stood in the middle of the table. Not only would they be able to meet their first monthly repayment to the bank but the future prosperity of Shipley Manor Country Club seemed assured. Only that was yesterday. Today, thanks to the *Shipley Gazette*, people had been calling to cancel their club memberships and demand their money back. Oh, and one or two had suggested that they should all be hung, drawn and quartered as well. Polly and the Captain came into the room.

'How's Tom's father?' inquired Seymour.

'Maggie's taking a look at him now,' replied the Captain. 'Hopefully it's nothing worse than a bump on the head. I have to say he seemed more concerned about his briefcase – I think we'd better do as he said and take a look inside it. Would you mind, Polly?'

Polly handed him the briefcase and he tipped the contents out on to the table. Sitting on top was the *Shipley Gazette*. Because Shipley Manor was out in the country, the Captain's copy hadn't yet been delivered. All he knew about it was what Tom had told him. As he picked up the newspaper, he could tell immediately that Tom hadn't been exaggerating. His mouth dropped open in amazement.

'Why in the Seven Seas would anyone write such terrible things about us?'

'See for yourself,' said Seymour, passing him Grub's 'Property Investments' file.

The Captain opened the file and there it was: proof that Barclay Grub and Venetia Pike were in partnership together, co-owners of the Shipley

Property Investment Company. And according to the evidence in the file, the Captain was just the latest in a long line of victims. He handed the file back to Seymour.

'So let me get this straight,' he said. 'The Council, or rather Venetia Pike, forced us to borrow money from the bank in order to carry out the improvements to Shipley Manor?'

Seymour nodded.

'Then they tried to wreck any chance we might have had of paying it back. I think we can assume that those snakes were *planted* in the kitchen so that we'd fail Mr Tutt's inspection –'

Polly suddenly jumped up. 'That's it!' she cried. 'It's the way they walk.'

'What do you mean, Polly?' asked the Captain.

'Matilda Goode, Venetia Pike and the woman I saw escaping up the driveway. They all had the same funny walk. Which means they're all the same person, just like in my dream.'

'That would certainly explain how the snakes got into the flour tin,' the Captain remarked. 'Venetia Pike has been a busy little bee, hasn't she?'

'I bet she's got a pretty nasty sting in her tail too,' muttered Edna.

'But we passed the inspection, didn't we?' Seymour continued. 'So then she and Grub sabotaged the fireworks to make sure that our grand reopening event would be a complete flop instead. And because that didn't work either, they've now cooked up this load of nonsense in the *Gazette*, so that they can close us down and make sure that all our new members will ask for their money back. Anything just so long as we end up broke and unable to pay off the loan.'

'I see,' said the Captain. 'So now Grub will give us a choice, won't he? Either hand Shipley Manor over to the bank, or sell it to him and Pike for much less than it's worth – just enough to enable us to repay the loan and go and live in a beach hut somewhere.'

'But that's blackmail!' protested Polly.

'Legal blackmail, I fear,' said Seymour, tapping the Captain's signature on the contract.

The Captain twiddled his beard, staring thoughtfully at the three glass jars on the table. There was still something he didn't understand.

'But surely we've made enough money from the food and drink sales alone to start paying them back?' he said to Seymour. 'Why can't we pay part of the loan back now, and raise the rest some other way – by selling the family silver, or marketing one or two of your inventions?'

'I don't know, Captain, but I think we'll find the answer in the loan contract.'

'Well, maybe we'll be all right then,' said the Captain more brightly. 'Let's take a look.'

He picked up the Shipley Bank loan contract.

'Right now, let's see – what did Tom's father say? Page eight, clause nine, subsection three.' He licked the tip of his finger and flicked through the pages. 'Ah, here it is. Jumping jellyfish, I'm going to need my magnifying glass to read this lot. Now where did I leave it?' He started to poke around in his beard.

'M for Montevideo, capital of Uruguay,' Polly reminded him.

'Thank you, Polly,' he said, locating the silver handle immediately. 'Now let's see. Ah yes, here we are – subsection three.'

> The party of the first part (Shipley Bank) will take full and immediate possession of the aforementioned property (Shipley Manor) if, for any reason whatsoever, the party of the second part (Captain Horatio Shipley) fails to repay its loan in full, to the aforesaid party of the first part (Shipley Bank), on the precise due date stipulated in this contract by the party of the first part's official representative (Mr B. Grub).

He sat back in his chair, and handed the contract to Seymour.

'Does that mean what I think it means, Seymour?'

'I'm afraid it does, Captain. Instead of allowing us to repay the loan bit by bit each month, as Grub promised, we have to pay it ALL back in one go, by –' He searched for the payment date written in the contract. '– *today*.'

Everyone in the room gasped. The Captain put his head in his hands and quietly asked one more question.

'How soon do you think these crooks will come knocking at our door, Seymour?'

Seymour studied the contract again.

'Ummmmmm well, according to this, the payment deadline is, er . . . twelve o'clock noon,' he said. 'So I think they'll strike then, before we have time to defend ourselves against all these lies.'

'Thank you, Seymour,' the Captain sighed. 'Well, Polly, it looks like I've steered us on to the rocks, doesn't it?'

But Polly didn't hear him. She was staring saucer-eyed at the *Gazette*, her face wet with tears.

Slowly she looked up. 'It's all my fault,' she sobbed. 'I told that nasty Venetia Pike woman all those things, about the children coming to stay in the summer, and about me having lessons at home and everything, and they've turned it all around to make it sound horrible.'

The Captain moved quickly to her side and crouched down beside her chair. He cupped her hands between his. 'Don't you dare blame yourself, Polly,' he said, squeezing them tightly. 'You did nothing wrong at all. Nothing. If anyone's to blame, it's me for signing that blessed contract in the first place. Here, wipe your eyes.'

He handed her a large white handkerchief. Polly took it and blew her nose with a loud honk.

'Let me guess,' said the Captain. 'A ship lost in the fog?'

Polly laughed.

'That's better,' he said. 'Right, let's go and see how the patient's getting along, shall we?'

In the kitchen, the news was slightly better. Maggie had checked Roger for broken bones and any other signs of serious injury. Then she and Tom had helped him into a chair so that she could clean and dress the wound on the back of his head. Finally, she had delivered her verdict.

'Everything's going to hurt for a while, Mr Sterling,' she said, 'but you're going to be fine.'

On her way out she had put a reassuring hand on Tom's shoulder. 'Just make sure he doesn't do any white-water rafting for a few days.'

When Maggie had gone, Tom made a cup of tea for his father and sat on the other side of the table watching him drink it. Suddenly it struck him how things had changed since the weekend. Here was he, sitting up smartly in his school uniform – clean shirt, straight tie, polished shoes – and there, slumped in the chair opposite him, was his father, wearing a black eye, a suit which looked as though he'd been mud-wrestling in it and a bandage round his head which pushed his hair up like a tuft of grass.

Roger could feel his strength gradually returning.

'How do I look?' he asked huskily.

'Like I did two nights ago,' replied Tom. 'Only much, much worse.'

A few minutes later Polly and the Captain rejoined them in the kitchen. Slugbucket had already returned, having drawn a blank in his search for Grub.

'How's the patient?' the Captain asked.

'Much better, thank you,' replied Roger. 'But I came to warn you. The Council is planning to do something terrible this afternoon.'

'Close us down, I know,' replied the Captain. 'This newspaper story is all the excuse they need.'

Roger shook his head grimly.

'I'm afraid it's much worse than that,' he said. 'They're sending in their Child Protection Team.'

Roger looked at their puzzled faces. He didn't want to explain what that meant in front of Polly, but time was running out fast. They had to know now.

'They're going to take the children away,' he said.

Roger's Revelation

Once, many years before, the Captain's ship had been caught in a storm. It was no ordinary storm. It arrived without warning, as if conjured up by some evil magician, and brought wild, roaring winds and mountainous waves crashing into the Captain's ship. With no time to outrun or avoid the storm, the Captain plotted a course straight into it. Day and night for three days the storm tore at the Captain's vessel with all its stinging fury, trying to overturn it or force it back. And day and night for three days the Captain stood his ground at the ship's wheel, slicing his ship straight and true through the storm's raging waters, like a sword aimed at its heart. Then, on the fourth day, as if it had suffered a mortal, puncturing blow, the storm weakened and died. The Captain emerged on the other side, having deviated not one degree from his course.

That same ship's wheel now stood in the conservatory at Shipley Manor, looking out over the valley down to the sea beyond. The Captain's grateful crew had presented it to him when he left the navy, and it was to this wheel that he came whenever he needed to think. He stood there now, in full uniform, turning the wheel slowly through his hands, exploring the different courses of action he could take. How could he steer Shipley Manor and its crew through the new storm that Venetia Pike was about to unleash against them? How could he protect Polly and Calypso? How could he keep the promise to his parents never to leave Shipley Manor? Finally, he set the wheel dead ahead. He had made his decision. He would not negotiate. He would not buckle. Whilst he still had breath in his body, neither Pike nor Grub would set their crooked, rotten feet inside Shipley Manor.

He turned as Slugbucket backed into the conservatory carrying a crate of Fizzle.

'They're all on their way up now, Captain,' Slugbucket told him, setting his clinking cargo down on the table, ''cept old Constance – says she'll stand watch in the Crow's Nest till Seymour gets back.'

'Is everything else ready?' the Captain asked.

''Tis, Cap'n. I've brought the chickens into the courtyard just in case we get stuck inside for a few days an' fancy an omelette, the port'oles is all shut tight an' the front door's locked and bolted. It's a good strong door is that – they'll need a batterin' ram to get past it.'

The Captain nodded. He put a hand on Slugbucket's shoulder.

'You know none of you has to stay, Slugbucket,' he said. 'If these people refuse to listen to reason, I've decided to fight them. Anyone who takes my side is likely to find themselves in big trouble.'

Slugbucket shook his head firmly. 'Nope, I ain't leavin', Cap'n,' he said. 'I reckons this is my fight as much as yourn. I've worked 'ere ever since I was knee 'igh to a ferret. First for yer grandfather, then yer father, bless 'is soul, and now you. This is where I belong, and you and Maggie and the children, well, you're the closest I got to family. I'm stayin' an' that's the end of it.'

The Captain smiled. 'And Seymour?' he asked.

''E feels the same as me, Cap'n.'

'I'd also like to help if I can,' called a voice from the door. Roger limped into the room followed by Tom and the others. 'Now that I know what's been going on, I'm sure I can persuade them to leave you alone. Once they see that I have the proof –' He patted the briefcase under his arm. '– they'll have to reconsider what they're doing.'

'I hope you're right, Roger,' replied the Captain. 'But in the meantime I think we should prepare for the worst. Shipmates!' He raised his voice so that they could all hear him. 'It seems that Venetia Pike and Barclay Grub will stop at nothing to get their hands on Shipley Manor. Because they fear we might now be able to pay off that wretched bank loan after all, they've decided not to take any chances. Under the cloak of her so-called Official Public Duty, it looks as though Pike intends taking Polly and Calypso into Council care. Once they are in her clutches, she will no doubt hold them hostage until I agree to surrender the estate to her and Mr Grub.'

'That's kidnappin',' said Slugbucket bitterly.

'It is indeed,' the Captain agreed. 'And Shipley Manor is the ransom. But after those headlines in the newspaper, Pike will have the whole of Shipley on her side, so no one will see it that way. I'm not sure how long it will take for the truth to come out, but until it does, one thing is certain. No one is going to lay so much as a finger on our children.'

'You can say that again,' Maggie declared quietly, drawing Polly and Calypso closer to her.

'Now,' the Captain continued, 'I want Maggie, Polly and Calypso to stay in the Crow's Nest with Seymour, Edna and Constance. You should be safe there, but if it looks as though these pirates are about to break into the house, I want you to move down to the cellar. No one will ever find those invisible doors, so you can hide in there until I come to get you out. I've left you enough food and drink for a couple of weeks, but I'm sure it won't come to that. Our young summer visitors are bound to come forward to refute those newspaper allegations and, together with the evidence in Roger's briefcase, we can soon expose Pike and Grub for the lying, cheating, sea slime they really are.'

Calypso gurgled approvingly at the Captain's plan.

'But I don't want to stay in the Crow's Nest,' protested Polly. 'I want to *do* something.'

The Captain knelt down to her. 'You can,' he promised. 'Seymour has a little present for our visitors which he'll need you to deliver for him.' Seymour leaned forward and whispered into Polly's ear. A contented smile spread across her face. Yes, that would do. The Captain stood up and continued.

'Roger and Tom, if you can talk some sense into these people, then please do, but I warn you, if they won't listen to reason, they're going to have to fight their way in, so please make sure you look after yourselves. Slugbucket, I'd like you to stay by the main door and make sure that no one comes in or out except us. Now, unless anyone has any questions, I think it's time to break out the Fizzle – we're going to need all the help we can get.'

The Captain reached into the crate and began to hand out bottles of Fizzle.

'I suppose Tom's told you that the water here is – how shall I put this? – rather special.'

'It's magical,' said Polly, then, looking at Tom, 'except some people round here won't believe me.'

'He did mention it, yes,' replied Roger. 'But I've always told him that there's no such thing as magic. It's what I've always believed – at least until today,' he added.

'And now?' asked the Captain.

'Well, after all that's happened I think I'm ready to believe that almost anything's possible,' said Roger. 'In the space of two days I've seen a whole country house disappear right in front of my eyes, I've discovered that the manager of Shipley Bank, my own boss, is not only a criminal but also seems capable of vanishing into thin air and now I look set to go into battle against the Council, the newspaper, the police and everyone else I used to trust.'

'In that case, I think you'd better try some,' said the Captain, holding a bottle out to him.

One of the many rules in the Sterling household was that they didn't drink straight from bottles, so instinctively Roger looked around for a glass. When none was forthcoming he took a delicate, tidy sip from the bottle. He raised his eyebrows slightly, then took a big gulp. Then another.

'Woaoaoh!'

Polly jumped up, triumphant. 'He's "Got the Fizzle", he's "Got the Fizzle"! Now do you believe me, Tom?'

Roger sat down shakily, gripping the edge of his chair as though it might suddenly take off.

Tom's mouth dropped open. Please no, not his father as well.

'But what does it *do*, Dad, how does it make you feel?'

His father seemed not to hear. For almost a minute he just stared ahead in a daze, wide-eyed and speechless.

Finally, as though a hypnotist had suddenly clicked his fingers, Roger blinked and came out of his trance.

'Well . . . let me put it this way, Tom,' he said, slowly. 'You know that happy, excited, tingly feeling you get when you unwrap a wonderful present, something you've always wanted?'

Tom nodded.

'Well, it's like that only a million times better,

because it feels like you've just been given –' He paused to take another sip, just to make sure. '– the whole world.'

Tom tried hard to imagine how that might feel.

'Perhaps I should try to explain,' said Seymour. 'The Fizzle is like a connection. When you drink it, it becomes part of your body just like other food and drink does. But the difference is that it's intelligent. It can read your innermost thoughts and desires. It feels what you feel, and wants what you want. Not only that, but the Fizzle inside you is connected to the Fizzle everywhere else, whether it's sitting there in the moat or flowing through the pipes. It all feels part of you, and you of it. And because it also evaporates into the air, and soaks into the earth, and is drunk by the birds and absorbed by the trees, you feel joined up with everything in nature, as though you're part of one enormous family. And that's why we know the Fizzle will always help us, because that's what families try to do.'

'Yes,' said Tom, 'but I still don't understand why you have to believe in magic to "Get the Fizzle".'

'Magic is just a word, Tom, to explain the unexplainable. What you have to believe is that anything's possible. Because that opens a kind of switch in your head. When the switch is ON, your mind is open, so the Fizzle can get in and mix with your thoughts and become part of you. And when it's OFF, your mind is closed to the whole idea of magic, like there's a big No Entry sign in your head. The Fizzle can't get to know you because it's not been invited. It just hangs around in your body like ordinary water.'

Tom shook his head. All these ideas were the complete opposite of what he'd always been taught: don't believe in anything unless there's a sensible, scientific explanation for it, or you can read about it in the newspapers, or it's Official. And where was the man who'd taught him these things? Who only that morning had banned him from setting foot in Shipley Manor ever again? Sitting there with a delirious smile on his face, obviously convinced that Fizzle had magical powers. Perhaps it was the bump on his father's head doing it. Or maybe it was just another one of Seymour's tricks, like the talking sheep. He didn't know what to think.

'The thing is, Tom,' Seymour continued, 'it's not like waving a magic wand. We never know how the Fizzle will help us or what it will do, and we recognise the need to work just as hard ourselves for what we want. But we know that if we stand firm against these scoundrels today, the Fizzle will do everything it can to help.'

Tom forced a stiff smile. Seymour could see that he wasn't convinced.

'Look,' he continued, 'I always wanted to be an entertainer, ever since I was your age. Even after my riding accident put me in this wheelchair, it was still my greatest wish. That's why I like entertaining the kids in the summer. Well, the Fizzle knew that, and the other night it gave me the chance to put on a great show in front of a thousand people. You can call it magic, or anything you like, but the fact is that it happened, and it fulfilled my dream, and without the Fizzle it wouldn't have been possible. It could do the same for you, Tom, but you're rejecting it, when all it wants to do is help you. You need to flip that switch in your head to ON, Tom.'

But Tom couldn't, even though he desperately wanted to. Everything he'd ever learned told him that some things were truly impossible, and that real magic was one of them. Magic was just one of those pretend words, like fairies and ghosts, which belonged in books and films, but not in the real world. He felt more confused than ever before. He'd come here today not sure where he belonged. Was it in the safe, sensible world of order and rules in which he'd always lived? Or was it at Shipley Manor, where everything felt so much more exciting and carefree? Now that his father had 'Got the Fizzle' too, both worlds had somehow joined together, leaving him stranded on the outside.

Now he was just a bewildered onlooker, the only person there who still didn't believe in magic. And no matter how much they wanted him to be part of the Fizzle, the switch in his head was still marked OFF.

'Come on in, the water's fine,' they were saying, but he couldn't take the plunge. He simply could not believe that *anything* was possible.

At that moment Constance Boff's frail voice called out from the Crow's Nest.

'Prepare to repel boarders, dear – our visitors have arrived.'

The Battle for Shipley Manor

The Chief Executive of Shipley Council glanced impatiently at her watch. That miserable little slime-ball was late again. Where could he be? As the seconds ticked away, Pike surveyed the formidable forces which she had gathered around her and which now stood by the gates, awaiting her instructions. The Council was represented by herself, the Council's Child Protection Team – who were there to respond to the overwhelming public demand for Polly and Calypso to be taken into care – and the head of the Council's Trading Standards Department, who had come to give formal notification to Captain Shipley that the Shipley Manor Country Club was now officially closed. The Chief Constable had provided four rather bored-looking policemen to oversee the proceedings, and the *Shipley Gazette* had sent along its finest reporter to record the event and write a follow-up story, provisionally entitled 'Shipley Manor Showdown'. Finally, there was Rufus Knuckles and his team of bailiffs, who Pike and Grub hired regularly to accompany Grub on his unofficial bank visits, and whose presence usually convinced his victims that their houses were about to be seized. Pike checked her watch once more. If he didn't turn up soon she'd do it her way. It always amazed her what parents would agree to if you threatened to take their children away. You'd think they'd be pleased to be rid of the puking, pint-sized parasites, wouldn't you? But no. Instead they would grovel and promise to do whatever it took to keep them. Well, Captain, today it's going to take another one of your signatures, this time on the bottom of a sale contract.

'Right, that's it,' she announced finally. 'He can catch up with us at the house.'

She began to lead her small army of unwitting accomplices down the driveway. Quite by accident, they soon found themselves marching in step like a platoon of soldiers, and one of the sheep, its curiosity aroused by the rhythmic crunching of their footsteps, ambled over to the fence to investigate. Seymour, back on watch in the Crow's

Nest, couldn't resist picking up the microphone and offering a sheepish welcome to the visitors.

'Hu-u-u-p tw-o-o-o-o thr-e-e-e fou-r-r-r, Hu-u-u-p tw-o-o-o-o thr-e-e-e fou-r-r-r,' he bleated as Pike marched past the sheep.

'Lamb chops,' she snapped back quick as a flash.

At the end of the driveway, Pike signalled for her colleagues to stop, then continued forward several paces.

'Captain Shipley,' she called out. The Captain, who had been watching her approach through the small hatch in the door, turned to his companions.

'I'd better find out what she has to say first,' he suggested. 'You never know your luck – she might be here to present us with the Country Club of the Year Award.' He stepped blinking into the bright sunlight, then waited for Slugbucket to bolt the door – clunk, clunk – behind him, before continuing to the middle of the drawbridge. Pike was there waiting for him, a sickly, sneering smile cracking her face.

'Remember me, ssssweetie?'

'Venetia Pike,' he replied. 'Or should I say Matilda Goode?'

'Well, aren't you the clever one?' she said. 'But it won't help you now, Captain Shipley. I'm here in my official capacity as Chief Executive of Shipley Council to issue you with a Child Protection

Order. No doubt you've read the papers – child slavery indeed, tut-tut-tut – you *have* been a naughty boy, haven't you?'

The Captain didn't say a word. He refused to be provoked.

She continued, 'You understand that under such circumstances the Council's clear duty is to take your two little –' She searched around for the right word, before spitting it out. '– *brats* into care. For their own protection, of course – the citizens of Shipley are expecting nothing less.'

Again the Captain remained silent. She still hadn't come to the point.

'There is, of course, one thing you can do to sssstop it happening,' she said, pulling a sheet of paper from her bag and handing him a pen. 'Sell Shipley Manor to me now and I can make all these people go away. Just ssssign this little piece of paper and, puff, they're gone.' She fluttered her hand in the air like a magician making something disappear. 'I'm the boss, you see, ssssweetie – top banana, SSSShe who Must be Obeyed.'

The Captain took the contract from her and started to read it. Under its terms, the Captain would sell the whole Shipley Manor estate to Pike and Grub for a tenth of what it was worth.

'Outrageous!' He tore the paper in half and handed it back to her. Then, for good measure, he snapped the pen in two and handed that back as well. 'We know all about your shady business dealings with Mr Grub, and we have enough proof to report you to the authorities,' he told her.

Pike threw her head back. 'Ha! We *are* the authorities, you fool. And no one's going to listen to you now, anyway.'

'We'll see about that,' he replied. 'In the meantime, you're not taking the children or the house. I've never abandoned ship in my life, madam, and I'm not about to do it for a wizened old stick insect like you. Now get off my property.'

The Captain regretted having to insult all the perfectly nice wizened old stick insects in the world, but his comment was well calculated. If he could provoke Pike into losing her temper, then perhaps she would make a mistake, reveal herself as the vicious schemer she most certainly was. It almost worked there and then. Pike's entire face erupted into uncontrollable twitching as she tried to contain her fury. Old! Wizened! Stick insect! No one spoke to her like that. She wanted to rip him open with her fingernails. But she wasn't about to give up her 'official' advantage by attacking him in front of four policemen, no matter how much he deserved it.

'Have it your own way, ssssweetie,' she hissed through clenched teeth. 'And I'll add wilful destruction of Council property to your list of offences.' Still trembling like a pressure cooker ready to blow its top, she dropped the broken pen back into her bag and pulled out the Child Protection Order. She held it top and bottom like a mediaeval scroll, and after taking a moment or two to compose herself, began to read aloud in a crisp, official voice.

'The Council is hereby empowered under the 1957 Child Protection Act to take Polly Seabright and Calypso Seabright into the care of Shipley Social Services Department.'

As soon as she had finished, she turned and marched off the drawbridge. Then the two Child Protection Officers stepped forward to carry out their official duty. The moment they put a foot on the drawbridge, the Captain's hand went to the hilt of his sword. Immediately they stopped in their tracks and two police constables moved in front of them – the day had suddenly become a whole lot more interesting. They took a step towards the Captain.

'Now come on, sir, there's no need for this to get out of hand,' said one of them.

They took another step forwards. At that moment Roger ran out of the door and placed himself between the Captain and the police. Bandaged, dirty and with his voice still rather weak, he didn't make the best spokesman, but he was determined to do whatever he could.

'You're making a big mistake,' he said breathlessly. 'That woman –' He wagged a dirty fingernail over their shoulders at Pike. '– and the manager of Shipley Bank have set this whole thing up – the newspaper article, everything – just so that they can get their hands on this estate. It's a property fraud, you see. Look, I've got all the evidence here in my briefcase.'

But before he could show them anything, one of the policemen took another step towards the Captain. Without thinking, Roger stepped forward too and tried to push him back.

'No, no, no, you don't understand.'

He might as well have been talking to a brick wall. In an instant his arm had been twisted behind his back and he was being marched off the drawbridge. He struggled, protesting the Captain's innocence and begging the policeman and the *Gazette* reporter to examine the evidence in his briefcase.

But the policeman was unmoved.

'Arrest him,' called Pike. 'Drunk and Disorderly. Assaulting a Police Officer. And no one is permitted to open that briefcase – it contains highly confidential documents belonging to the Council.'

Then Tom appeared in the doorway and, before

the Captain could stop him, rushed over the drawbridge to help his father, only to be caught by the second policeman. Frantically he tried to wriggle free from the policeman's vice-like grip.

'My father's not drunk, and *he's* the one who's been assaulted. Let me go! *Let me go!*'

The two other policemen now stepped forward to negotiate with the Captain. Pike turned to the head bailiff.

'Rufus, get your men ready to go in behind them as soon as they disarm that buffoon.'

'Right you are, Miss Pike. Come on then, lads, you heard what the lady said.'

'Come on then,' the Captain challenged them. 'Six against one – what are you waiting for?'

They took a step closer. He hadn't yet drawn his sword. Perhaps they could rush him.

'Now I'm sure you don't want anyone to get hurt, do you, sir?'

They inched forward, preparing to pounce. At that moment the whole drawbridge shook, as Slugbucket jumped down from the treadmill with a loud, dusty thud. He brushed himself off and planted himself alongside the Captain, arms crossed, legs apart. He greeted the policemen – 'Af'ernoon, gen'lemen, noice day' – before tilting his head towards the Captain.

'Thought I better come out this way, Cap'n,' he

explained through the side of his mouth, 'so's I could leave the door locked on the inside. Sorry I let Tom through – he ran out 'fore I knew what was 'appenin'.'

Slugbucket then called out to the policeman holding Roger.

'Mister Sterlin' over there's right, ye know. You've all been 'ad for fools, the lot o' yer. That woman's the only crook round 'ere. All you got to do is listen to what Mr Sterlin' 'as to say.'

But the policemen didn't want to know. They'd heard it all before. Still they hesitated. Slugbucket was a mountain of a man, and the Captain was armed – perhaps they should call for reinforcements?

Pike's impatience finally got the better of her.

'Go on, constable,' she ordered. 'Get them, get them, get th –'

Her voice tailed off as all eyes turned towards the track. A screaming silver blob had appeared suddenly from out of the woods. Barclay Grub had returned.

Dripping with slugs and half-blinded by the encrusted slime which cocooned him from head to toe, he zigzagged wildly towards them, his arms outstretched in front of him like an ant's feelers.

Slugbucket leaned towards the Captain. 'Well,

'oo'd a' thought it?' he said quietly. ''E must 'ave fallen into the slugpit when 'e attacked Mr Sterling. Spat 'im out again by the looks of it.'

Slugbucket was right. Moments after they had rescued Roger, the slugs decided that Grub was just too disgusting to share their pit. They had lifted him up, carried him to the edge on a huge sluggy wave and dumped him back on the ground. Perhaps it was the after-shave. Either way, the experience had left Barclay Grub stark raving mad, and for an hour he'd run around in the woods totally lost, bouncing from tree to tree like a silver ball in a pinball machine. Finally he had heard shouting and followed the noise. The first person he recognised through his mucus mask was Roger. 'Sterrrrliiiing!' he gurgled. He couldn't remember why, but he knew there was some reason he had to kill Roger and grab his briefcase. Screaming wildly, he hurled himself straight at him, clamping his oozing, sticky hands around Roger's neck and shaking him backwards and forwards. Roger dropped the case just as a third policeman wrestled Grub to the ground.

'Get off me, get off me! Don't you know who I am?' he howled at the policeman kneeling on his back. Then he fell silent as a pair of bright red stiletto shoes appeared just inches away from his nose. He didn't know why, but he was overjoyed to see them, like long-lost friends paying a surprise visit. But they weren't there to see him. They were there for the briefcase which lay on the ground beside him.

'I think I'd better take that,' Pike said, bending down to pick it up. As her bony hands reached for the handle, Grub reached out for her. Instinctively she jumped back, and as she did so the reporter from the *Shipley Gazette* took the opportunity to pick the briefcase up himself. Pike was livid.

'Give that to me!' she snapped, before managing to control herself. 'Really, there's nothing of interest in it – just boring Council paperwork.'

But the reporter pretended not to hear. Pike's barely disguised desperation to obtain the briefcase baffled him, and his reporter's nose was starting to sniff a good story. He turned to Roger, still held firm by the policeman, despite being bent double and gasping for breath after Grub's attack. 'Do you still want me to take a look inside your briefcase?' he asked.

Roger nodded, so the reporter opened the case and started to examine its contents. Pike watched him anxiously. If there really was some evidence in there, it wouldn't take him long to find it. She would have to act quickly, to get hold of those children while everyone was still on her side. She flicked the reporter an icy 'I'll fix you later' glance, then turned to the bailiffs.

'Right, Mr Knuckles,' she barked. 'It's high time you earned your money. I want you to help the policeman arrest those two fools on the drawbridge and take possession of Shipley Manor right now. There are children in there who need our help.'

The bailiff didn't move.

'No disrespect, Miss Pike,' he replied, 'but me and the lads weren't hired to take part in no sword fight.'

'We'll pay you double,' Pike offered desperately.

'The answer's still no, sorry.'

Pike looked around wildly. She was going to get into that house if it was the last thing she ever did. Then she saw the mechanical digger. It was parked a short way up the track next to the burned-out shed, where Slugbucket's caravan used to be. Almost unnoticed, except by Grub – whose hand she spiked with her stiletto heel on the way past – she leaped into the digger and turned the key. The machine spluttered into life, coughing dark clouds of exhaust fumes into the air like smoke signals. She looked down at the four control levers in front of her and decided to pull the nearest. Instantly the digger lurched forwards in a series of stuttering kangaroo hops.

'Get out of the way!' she cried. 'I'm coming through.' As she neared the drawbridge she called out to Rufus, 'Follow behind me and I'll clear a path for you.'

The fourth policeman was still on the edge of the drawbridge facing the Captain. But as soon as he saw Pike approaching he leaped out of the way. Pike halted the digger and started to pull the other control sticks backwards and forwards. The mechanical arm swung around wildly. The Captain and Slugbucket ducked and weaved as the huge metal fist punched the air around them, conscious that the slightest contact could kill them or knock them headlong into the moat. But still they stood firm. No one was going to get across that drawbridge.

Suddenly Pike changed her tactics. Instead of swinging the digger arm from side to side, she raised it above their heads, intending to crash it down on top of them. But she hadn't yet mastered the controls, and her first attempt missed the drawbridge completely, slamming the digger arm into the moat with an enormous crack. The Fizzle hissed around it in protest. Pike lifted the arm out of the water and tried again, but with a similar result. Finally, she decided that the only way to dislodge the Captain and Slugbucket would be to drive the digger straight at them. Then she could continue over the drawbridge and smash the doors down.

Screaming at Rufus and his men to follow her, Pike yanked on the controls. The digger jerked forwards to the edge of the drawbridge, just as a jet of water smashed into her chest, throwing her back in her seat and bringing the digger to a sudden halt. She looked up and there was Polly, directing the water from the top of the Crow's Nest, much as she had done the night of the Fizzlework display. Pike pushed herself forward against the water and managed to grab hold of the steering wheel. It wasn't over yet. She was about to move the digger forward again when Polly raised her aim and scored a direct hit, shooting Pike's blonde wig right off her head, like a marksman shooting a tin can off a wall. Horrified, Pike clutched her exposed scalp and let out a wild, ear-splitting scream. She leaped out of the digger and hurled herself at the Captain, clawing and scratching at him like a crazed fighting cock. As Slugbucket turned to pull her away, Rufus Knuckles and his men took the opportunity to jump on him from behind. He swung himself around, brushing two of them away like flies, but they were soon back, trying to drag him down. For a moment or two it looked as though he could carry all four of them, but finally his knees gave way and he crumpled to the floor under their combined weight. The moment he fell, the Captain pushed Pike aside and rushed over to help him. But no sooner had he reached down to pull the first bailiff off his friend's back than Pike flew at him again, this time gouging four deep furrows down his face with her blood-red fingernails. Seeing that was too much for Polly to bear. Before Maggie could stop her, she had grabbed her Fizzlestick and leaped on to the slide.

Tom and Roger watched helplessly as events unfolded. The policemen were still holding them well out of the way, uncertain whether or not they posed a threat to public safety. Their two colleagues were also fully occupied: one pinning a dangerous, oozing bank manager to the ground with the sole of his boot, the other trying to tame an unruly mechanical digger which the Chief Executive of Shipley Council had recklessly abandoned with its engine running. They had called for reinforcements, of course, but these would be some time in coming. In the meantime the battle for Shipley Manor seemed to have escalated, and they, along with the Council workers who watched open-mouthed from a safe distance, could do little about it.

'I think you should let them go,' a voice said. It was the reporter. He snapped the briefcase shut and delivered his verdict to the policemen.

'From the evidence in here,' he told them, 'I'm pretty sure that Mr Sterling and his son are telling the truth. These child slavery accusations have probably been cooked up by our slimy friend there

–' He tipped his head in Grub's direction. '– and that deranged woman on the drawbridge. They're the real villains. I'd watch out for her if I were you,' he added, having seen Pike line her fingernails with the Captain's blood. The two policemen glanced at each other, then nodded in silent agreement. Tom and Roger were free. But they could do no more than look on in horror as Polly, alone and unprotected, stepped out on to the drawbridge.

Pike sensed her presence immediately. She looked around. At last, this was her chance. If she could snatch Polly, then the Captain would have to sell the house to get her back. She looked around for the Council's Child Protection Team. Why weren't they coming to do their job? And why were they staring at her as if she were a lunatic? Gormless fools. Did she have to do *everything* herself? She stepped towards Polly, smiling like an old friend, ready to grab her as soon as she was within arm's reach. But Polly wasn't fooled. She edged backwards, her Fizzlestick raised defensively in front of her.

'And what's that supposed to be? A magic wand?' Pike sneered, moving closer. 'Well, you're not going to make *me* disappear.' As she lunged at Polly, a voice screamed at her from inside the house, 'Get your hands off my daughter,' and Maggie hurtled out of the darkness like an express train out of a tunnel. She slammed into Pike with such force that the two of them flew off the drawbridge and into the moat.

Magic

As Pike hit the surface, the Fizzle convulsed as if she were pure poison. It hissed and foamed in an allergic reaction, forcing itself away from her in a frenzied effort to escape. Like a dog trying to outrun its own tail, it began to flow around the house, dragging Pike and Maggie along with it. Within moments they had been swept away from the drawbridge and beyond the reach of Polly's outstretched Fizzlestick. At the same time the water level started to rise, as millions of gallons of Fizzle surged through cracks in the moat floor, summoned up from deep underground reservoirs to dilute Pike's toxic presence. As the churning waters sent Fizzlefish pirouetting into the air like performing dolphins, the Captain threw down his sword and plunged in after them.

By the time he came up for air, Pike and Maggie had disappeared around the first bend in the moat and water had already begun to swirl over the drawbridge. As it reached the bailiffs, they abandoned Slugbucket and retreated to higher ground. Immediately Slugbucket leaped back on to his feet and scooped Polly into his arms. He tried to pass her through the doorway to Edna, but she refused to go, pressing both hands and feet against the door frame and protesting wildly.

'I'm not leaving them,' she yelled. 'I'm not going inside until I know they're all right.'

There was no time to argue. The water had already started to flow in through the open doorway and they had to close it fast.

'Bolt the door, Edna,' said Slugbucket. 'She'll be safe enough on the treadmill.'

As the heavy oak door clunked shut behind them, Slugbucket hoisted Polly on to the port treadmill and took the Fizzlestick from her.

'Now you climb right ter the tarp, you 'ear,' he ordered, wagging his finger, 'an' don't come down 'less I says so.'

As Polly started climbing, he waded knee-deep across the drawbridge and grasped the rim of the other treadmill, ready to hook Maggie and the Captain to safety as soon as the water brought them back around the house. 'An' Pike as well, I s'pose,' he muttered to himself grudgingly. 'Not that she deserves it.'

On the other side of the moat Tom and his father had watched helplessly as the water surged over the bank and spread towards them. But as the police and bailiffs scurried around looking for ropes or anything else that could be thrown into the water, Tom realised that there was something he had to do, even though the thought of it terrified him.

'Dad, you've got to help me get to the digger.'

His father looked puzzled. 'What on earth for?'

'Because I can stretch the arm into the moat and save them,' Tom replied. 'I know how to operate it – Polly taught me.'

Suddenly Roger was overcome with fear. Tom's mother had drowned whilst saving a man's life, and now here was Tom, who couldn't swim a stroke, wanting to take the same risk. It was as though history was trying to repeat itself. Well, he wouldn't let it, Fizzle or no Fizzle. As memories of that awful day flooded into his head like liquid pain, he found himself saying no.

But Tom persisted. 'Please, Dad, trust me – I know I can do it.'

Roger bit his lip nervously and looked across at the digger, squatting half-submerged on what used to be the edge of the moat, its headlights protruding above the swirling water like a hippo's nostrils. Although the water hadn't yet reached the engine it soon would, and then it would be too late. It was now or never.

He took hold of Tom's arm and led him into the water. Barely had it reached their knees before the current started to pull at their legs, inviting them into its grip more and more insistently with every stride. As it grew deeper and stronger, they turned themselves sideways against the current, edging crab-like towards the back of the digger. By the time they reached it, the water was up to Tom's waist and threatening to sweep him off his feet, and it was only Roger's firm grip that kept him upright. Roger helped Tom on to the back of the digger.

'Be as quick as you can,' he said, 'and when I say we go, we go – agreed?'

Tom nodded and clambered over the machine to the driver's seat. He turned the key. Nothing. He tried again.

'Come on – come *onnnnn*!'

This time the engine roared into life. For a few seconds the digger flexed its arm like a one-armed body builder – left and right, forward and back, up and down – as Tom reminded himself of the controls. Then he was ready to begin. Slowly and carefully he extended the digger arm over the moat and began to lower it down to the surface. He knew that if he dipped the arm too far into the water the fierce current might sweep it away and take him and the digger with it. On the other hand, if it was too high the Captain or Maggie might not be able to reach it. It had to be just right. But Polly had taught him well, and with Slugbucket guiding him down from the other side of the moat, the digger arm was soon positioned just a few inches above the surface. Perfect. Now all he had to do was open up the huge mechanical jaws and get ready to catch.

The second the jaws locked into position, Polly called to Tom from the top of the treadmill, and he turned to see Maggie, Pike and the Captain reappear from the side of the house. As the swirling white water bundled them towards the drawbridge, Slugbucket reached out with Polly's Fizzlestick and hooked Maggie in like a prize fish, pulling her, gasping and coughing, on to the treadmill. At the same time, Pike and the Captain swept past him and clunked into the digger arm. The sudden, bruising impact slowed them down for no more than an instant, but in that time the Captain managed to clasp his hands around the cold metal edge of one of the jaws and hold on tight. Pike wasn't so successful, and despite her clawing protests the water tore her away from the digger. As she swept past the Captain she reached out one last time, digging her fingernails deep into his ankles.

The Captain tightened his grip and held firm, gritting his teeth against the pain and straightening his body in an effort to streamline himself against the current. Then he heard Tom calling out to him.

'Hang on, Captain, I'm going to move you across to the treadmill.'

With his eyes half closed against the onrushing water, the Captain felt a sudden jolt as the digger arm started its short journey across the moat. Another jolt told him that it had stopped. He looked up to see Slugbucket hanging off the treadmill, his free hand reaching out to him.

'The digger arm won't go no further, Cap'n – you'll 'ave to grab my 'and.' The Captain nodded in reply. 'Roight then,' yelled Slugbucket. 'On the count o' three: one, two –'

With Pike still hanging on to him by her fingernails, the Captain launched himself at Slugbucket. Instantly the current re-established its authority and tried to sweep the two of them away from the treadmill. But Slugbucket was too quick for it, and as the Captain reached out a huge hand locked around his wrist. Holding on firmly to the treadmill, Slugbucket then started to pull the Captain to safety. Pike's extra weight made progress slow, and with her presence whipping the Fizzle around her into such a helpless frenzy, Slugbucket found himself weakening. Gradually he began to lose his tug of war with the current, but just as the Captain's hand started to slip from his grasp there was a sudden shriek and Pike plunged back into the water, leaving ten broken fingernails embedded, like flaming red thorns, in the back of the Captain's trousers.

Slugbucket tightened his grip on the Captain and pulled him to safety, while the raging current carried Pike over the drawbridge. Then Maggie's scream rang out above the roar of the water – 'No, Polly, noooooooo' – as Polly reached out to Pike from the bottom of the other treadmill. As Pike swept past she grabbed Polly's hand, pulling her instantly into the water. Instinctively the Captain tried to jump after them, but Slugbucket held him back.

'You won't last two minutes, Cap'n. I'll go,' he said handing him the Fizzlestick. 'Jus' be ready fer next time she comes round.'

Tom watched from the digger as Slugbucket ripped off his jacket and prepared to jump. Why was he hesitating? Then he saw why. Slugbucket's caravan had appeared round the bend, spinning and bucking wildly as it tried to unseat the fluffy white cat, which was clinging to its roof like a terrified rodeo rider. As it sped past him Slugbucket took an enormous leap and landed on the top step. He reached inside the door and pulled out a length of rope. Polly wasn't far ahead – perhaps it would reach her.

'Polly', he cried. 'Get ready to catch!'

As they disappeared around the side of the house, Roger leaned over the digger and shook Tom's arm. The water was now up to his chest, and he was having to lean hard against the current to stop himself from being swept away.

'Tom, we have to go *now*.'

But Tom couldn't. He had one more thing to do.

'I've got to move the digger arm out of the way, Dad. If I don't, the caravan will smash into it next time round, the water's rising so fast.'

His father nodded sharply. As Tom pulled on the controls, the arm lifted into the air and swung round towards the bank. Then the water finally reached the engine and it spluttered to a halt. That was it. Roger pulled Tom over his shoulders and headed back to the shore, angling himself against the current. As his father struggled through the water, Tom looked back at the house hoping to catch sight of Polly, but she and Slugbucket had disappeared from view.

Then he saw it. As he scanned the moat his gaze fell on the giant wooden octopus, Polly's favourite diving platform. The water hadn't yet been strong enough or deep enough to sweep the huge oak-root away, but now it was starting to shift, becoming lighter and more buoyant with every second. Tom watched as it slid, silently and unnoticed, into the main current. As it did so, its long tentacles appeared to soften and move freely. And as they glistened in the sun like wet skin, Tom no longer saw a tree-root at all. He saw a real octopus. Tom decided at once that this was no deception, no trick of the light – this was real magic. He cupped his hands and gulped down a mouthful of Fizzle.

As the feeling of oneness spread through his body he knew that the water wasn't his enemy at all: it was part of him now, just as it was part of Polly. As the Fizzle merged with his thoughts he started to feel hers too. Like two drops in the same pond, he and Polly had become connected. The first thing he could tell was that Slugbucket hadn't managed to reach her. She was still in the water with Pike, and every few seconds he sensed a surge of fear and panic as Pike forced her beneath the surface in her desperate effort to stay afloat. Worst of all, he could feel Polly's thoughts becoming fainter, as the struggle with Pike drove her to exhaustion. He had to save her.

He closed his eyes to concentrate on that single, undiluted thought and felt a sudden rush of confidence as the millions of gallons of water spinning round the house instantly shared it with him. Even though he couldn't swim, he knew that the Fizzle would protect him. As a chain of policemen reached out to his father, Tom twisted out of his grasp and threw himself into the water. Roger lunged after him, but the current knocked his legs away like skittles and he fell sideways. By the time he looked up, Tom was well beyond his reach and two policemen were hauling him, struggling and protesting, out of the water. As the rising water forced them further and further up the slope, they could do nothing but watch as Tom was sucked into the white, foaming swirl that encircled the house. Then, as the valley echoed to Roger's despairing howl, Tom disappeared beneath the surface.

As the water folded over his head Tom knew he was doing the right thing. The more he had struggled to stay afloat the more the Fizzle had tried to pull him down, and the effort was exhausting him. He realised that he needed to trust the Fizzle, to believe that it would take care of him. And so, with one last gulp of air, he had let it take him.

Immediately he sank deep into the moat, where the current was at its strongest and most turbulent. As it sped him around the house he was buffeted on all sides by jets of Fizzle which surged up through the cracks in the moat floor and flipped him this way and that like a feather caught in a raggedy breeze. Then, almost before he realised it, he was out of breath, and his lungs were starting to burn. What should he do? Suddenly he was distracted by an itch on his upper lip. Instinctively his hand went to scratch it, but then something told him not to. Two Fizzle bubbles, no bigger than grains of sand, had settled on it and become one. Then more joined them, so that within seconds thousands had united to form a single apple-sized bubble over his mouth. And not a moment too soon. As his lungs felt ready to burst, he opened his mouth and sucked in the precious gas. It tasted a bit odd, but the small, shallow breath was enough to keep Tom going until a larger bubble had formed. He breathed that in too, and this time he was able to hold his breath for longer. The next time he breathed, the bubble was large enough to fill his lungs, and so it went on. Very soon the bubble had grown so large that it covered his head like a deep-sea diver's helmet and he could breathe normally.

As his thoughts returned to saving Polly, he realised that she could be on the opposite side of the moat, and that they could spin around the house all day without ever meeting up. The best thing to do would be to anchor himself against something solid and wait for the current to bring her round to him. As he completed his first circuit of the moat he saw the drawbridge looming up ahead. It was some way above him, but as the water carried him underneath he kicked hard off the moat floor and hit the underside. Before he could be swept away he reached out and grabbed hold of the edge, then hung on as the current stretched him out like a windsock in a hurricane. As the water surged over him he realised that he could use its power to his advantage, so he dragged his upper half over the edge of the drawbridge and on to the top. Immediately he felt as though he was being cut in half as the water tried to force him both sides of the wood. But he was perfectly balanced, and as he turned to face the current it pinned his back hard against the edge of the drawbridge and held him steady. Now where was Polly? He estimated that it had taken him less than a minute to complete one full circuit of the house, in which case Polly could arrive at any moment. He peered ahead, searching, waiting. Then, just as a Fizzlefish flashed past him in a blur of luminous orange, she was there.

But she was not alone. Pike was still holding on to her, pushing her repeatedly under the water in her own desperate effort to stay afloat. Tom watched helplessly as Polly's arms and legs whipped up a frenzy of silver bubbles, but failed to wrench her free from Pike's grasp. Then, as two eagle-like hands clamped themselves over Polly's shoulders and pushed her down one last time, she stopped struggling. As her eyes drooped shut and her seemingly lifeless body began to sink, Pike discarded her like an unwanted rag-doll, and Tom was able to reach up and pluck her from the current. As Pike continued on over his head, Tom pulled Polly down close to him so that their noses were almost touching inside the bubble. With the water now pressing them together against the drawbridge, he gripped her arms and shook her.

'Polly! Polly!'

Suddenly she gasped, and as millions of new bubbles streamed in to feed her greedy appetite, Polly gulped down huge, delicious lungfuls of the gas from Tom's personal supply. Finally she opened her eyes.

'You "Got the Fizzle",' she observed weakly. ''Bout time too.'

Tom managed a weak smile, but the pain across his back had become so unbearable that he was desperate to find a way out of the water.

To his right he could see the digger, lying submerged like a giant pincered crab on what used to be the edge of the moat. To his left, next to the house, the starboard treadmill arced down through twenty feet of water, with only the barest sliver remaining above the surface. This was their best way out. Maggie and the Captain would still be on top looking out for Polly, and if he and Polly could reach them they would all be able to escape on to the roof.

So, with the current gluing Polly to him, he began to inch sideways along the edge of the drawbridge. As soon as he was within arm's reach of the treadmill, he instructed Polly to wrap her arms and legs around him like a baby monkey. Then he started to haul himself and her up the metal framework. He climbed slowly, aware that any slip could see them thrust back into the main current or, worse still, hurled painfully or even fatally into the port treadmill on the opposite side of the drawbridge. But gradually, the moat's swirling white surface drew closer and closer until Tom's hand broke through and gripped the Captain's ankle. Immediately the Captain reached down and hauled Polly out of the water. Then he held out his hand for Tom. But instead of taking it, Tom hesitated. He could see his father calling to him from the other side of the water. Like Polly and the Captain, he was telling him to climb to safety. But instead, as Slugbucket's caravan reappeared from the other side of the house, Tom pushed away from the treadmill and grabbed the back wheel as it sped past. His arm was almost wrenched off, but a huge hand quickly plucked him out of the foam and dumped him, dripping, on to the top step.

'Slugbucket,' Tom gulped, pulling himself to his feet. 'I have to get back to my dad. It's where I belong.'

Slugbucket nodded understandingly.

'Oi tell you what, Tom, nex' time round we'll throw a rope ter shore an' maybe they can pull us near enough for you to jump. 'Ere, tie this to one o' the wheels.'

As Slugbucket handed Tom one end of the rope, he wound the rest into a series of tight loops. Then, as they came back round to the drawbridge, Slugbucket leaned out and threw the rope towards the shore. It fell short, but as Roger threw himself into the water he caught it and slowed the caravan long enough for others to join him. As the final bailiff lent his weight to the effort, the caravan slowed to a stop and the rope sprang up like a tightrope. It was still too far for Tom to jump, so he crossed his legs over the rope and pulled himself along upside down. Finally, he swung down in front of his father and called back to Slugbucket.

'Come on, it's easy.'

But Slugbucket shook his head. He also knew where he belonged.

'I'm stayin',' he shouted back. 'Let go o' the rope.'

On the count of three they granted Slugbucket his wish, and as the caravan shot back into the current, Tom and Roger stumbled backwards towards the shore. As soon as they cleared the water Roger threw his arms around his son in relief. This time Tom wasn't embarrassed – instead, he closed his watery eyes and hugged his father back.

'You're daft and brave at the same time, just like your mother,' his father whispered in his ear. 'She'd be so proud of you, Tom.'

Despite being soaked to the skin with cold water, Tom suddenly felt flooded with warmth, as though he were back on that hot, sunny beach with his mother, building their sandcastle. He didn't want the moment to end, but when he opened his eyes and looked up, he found that Polly and the others were still in terrible danger. Although they had managed to climb from the treadmill on to to the roof, the water had continued to rise. And whilst the strong portholes and thick foam-filled walls had, until now, kept it out of the building, millions of gallons were poised to flood over the roof and into the courtyard, filling Shipley Manor like a bucket. As the rising water pushed Tom and Roger further and further up the slope, so too the Captain, Maggie and Polly could only retreat to the final sanctuary of the Crow's Nest. From there, with Edna, Calypso, Seymour and Constance, they looked down helplessly as the water edged its way across the roof. But then, just as the first few drops began to trickle into the courtyard, the air around Shipley Manor started to rumble. Instinctively

Tom looked skyward, expecting to see a dark thunderstorm brewing. But the sky was clear blue, and as the rumble grew louder and the ground beneath him began to shake, Tom realised that the sound wasn't coming from above him at all. It was coming from below.

Suddenly, as a clamour of rooks fled squawking from the treetops, the air erupted with the deep, thunderous roar of a mountain being torn in half, and Shipley Manor, foundations and all, parted company with the ground. It rose majestically out of the water, seeming to defy gravity for a moment as it hung, motionless, above the surface. Then it crashed back down, sending a huge wave rolling out in all directions in an ever-expanding circle. As police and bailiffs scattered uphill to escape it, Tom and his father ran to the woods and climbed to the safety of Polly's Perch. As the wave broke over the tree-trunk below them they looked out to see the house rise up a second time. But this time there was no wave. Instead, the house settled back in the water and floated. With its huge metal treadmills licking the surface, Shipley Manor had, amazingly, been transformed into a magnificent stone paddle-steamer.

But its troubles were far from over. As it was wrenched out of the earth, the house had left a gaping hole behind it, and as water spiralled down to quench its thirst, Shipley Manor found itself in the centre of a massive whirlpool which threatened to suck it down and engulf it. No longer anchored to the ground, the house slowly began to rotate. As the view from the Crow's Nest moved round in front of him, the Captain realised that their only chance of survival was to break out of the whirlpool and join the millions of gallons of Fizzle which were now flooding down the valley. But how? As he looked around for inspiration he spotted Tom signalling to him from Polly's Perch. He was spinning his arms around like propellers, then stopping them, then spinning them the other way.

'Reverse the treadmills!' he was screaming. 'Reverse the treadmills!'

But no one in the Crow's Nest could hear him above the roar of the water. No one, that is, except Polly. Somehow she could hear him as clearly as if he were standing inside her head.

'He's telling us to reverse the treadmills, Captain,' she told him confidently.

The Captain looked at her, puzzled momentarily. Then Seymour clapped his hands.

'Of course!' He reached for the blowpipe and called out across the water, 'Brilliant idea, Tom. Thank you.'

Within seconds Seymour had dispatched Maggie and Polly to the cellar, where they found themselves ankle deep in water. Polly guessed correctly that it had leaked in through the two holes which connected the generator to the treadmills, but as Shipley Manor was no longer under water the flow had stopped. Instead, two shafts of light cut down through the darkness, illuminating the generator room. Polly and Maggie splashed across to the generator and positioned themselves either side. The springs in the corners of the room were coiled up tight, ready to release their power. But instead of releasing it into the generator, the idea was to divert it back outside to the treadmills, turning them like the paddles on a paddle-steamer. At least that was the plan. Whether they would be strong enough to push Shipley Manor out of the whirlpool was anybody's guess. As the Captain stood at the ship's wheel in the conservatory and prepared to issue orders over the blowpipe, he knew he had to choose exactly the right moment to break free. The house would have to be facing the valley with the current pushing it along from behind. Then just before it swung them back round, he would use a sudden burst of treadmill power to divert them out of the whirlpool. Once out of its grip Shipley Manor would join the rest of the water cascading down the valley towards the sea. But he would have to be quick: with every passing second the whirlpool sucked them faster and deeper into its centre.

Then at last the moment came. The Captain snatched up the blowpipe and bellowed into the funnel, 'Full ahead both engines,' and Polly and Maggie switched the levers on the generator to REVERSE. Immediately, in a blur of spinning cogs and pulleys, the power surged back into the treadmills and they started to turn. A white, gurgling froth appeared behind the house as the treadmills sped up and bit into the water, edging Shipley Manor away from the centre of the whirlpool. As it veered slightly to the right, the Captain gave the order 'Port stop' and Maggie stopped her treadmill momentarily, leaving Polly to nudge the house back into position. Then, as it turned back to face the sea, the command 'Ahead both engines' rang out again, and with one final push, Shipley Manor broke free of the whirlpool and joined the water flooding down the valley. The Captain did his best to steer a straight course, but it was obvious that the Fizzle was in charge. As water surged underneath to raise Shipley Manor well clear of the ground, the Captain could do little except order his crew to hold tight and prepare for the ride of their lives.

As the house cleared the end of the Shipley Manor estate and headed into open countryside, the valley floor dropped away sharply and Shipley

Manor went into free fall. It plunged towards the sea on a huge liquid roller-coaster, swinging wildly from left to right and banking steeply on its sides as it rode the valley walls to avoid everything in its path. As the water lifted the house over high stone walls and fences in a succession of stomach-churning peaks and troughs, so too it spun and twisted around numerous obstacles in a dizzying display of power and control. Either side of the house, huge plumes of spray exploded into the air as Fizzle smashed into trees and telegraph poles just inches away from the walls. Inside, the Captain and his crew clung on as books flew around their heads like demented bats and invisible hands plucked knives out of drawers and hurled them quivering into door frames. Then, just as the Captain was wondering how much longer they could survive inside this human cocktail shaker, the mouth of the valley opened wide in front of them, and they started to slow down.

As the ground levelled out, the Fizzle spread itself smooth and flat, gently turning Shipley Manor bow first to meet the sea. Then finally, the journey was over, and as a dozen Fizzlefish skimmed ahead in bright formation, Shipley Manor was delivered like a baby into its new world.

The Captain had come home.

Voices

'Tom, can you hear me?'

'Polly! Where are you?'

'We're on the sea. Where are you?'

'I'm still on the perch with Dad.'

'You should be able to see us from there, Tom.'

'All I can see is two dots on the horizon, one big, one little.'

'That's us! We're the big one and Slugbucket's caravan will be the little one. He followed us all the way down the valley with Nautipus stuffed down the front of his jacket.'

'Amazing!'

'Not half as amazing as being able to talk to each other like this.'

'I know, something must have happened when

we were breathing the Fizzle gas together.'

'Like magic, you mean, Tom?'

'If you like.'

'Does your dad know you're talking to me?'

'No, he can't tell. We're just sitting here watching the policemen search for Pike. The last time anyone saw her she was wrestling with the octopus. How about you?'

'I'm with the Captain sucking a gigantic gobstopper. We're looking at maps.'

'Maps of where?'

'Everywhere. The Captain says we deserve a holiday, so we're choosing where to go. What will you do, Tom?'

'Go back to school, I suppose, like normal.'

'Couldn't you and your dad come with us instead?'

'I don't know. Hang on, I'll ask him a "What if?" question.'

'Well, what did he say?'

'He said remember the new family motto.'

'I didn't know you had one.'

'We do now.'

'So what is it?'

A deep, relaxed smile spread across Tom's dirty face.

'Anything's possible,' he said.

Acknowledgements

My thanks go to Ruth Alltimes, Darren Nash, my wife Jo and my children Jessica, Sarah and Samuel for their invaluable help and encouragement during the writing of this book.